Are You
Being Served?

THE INSIDE STORY

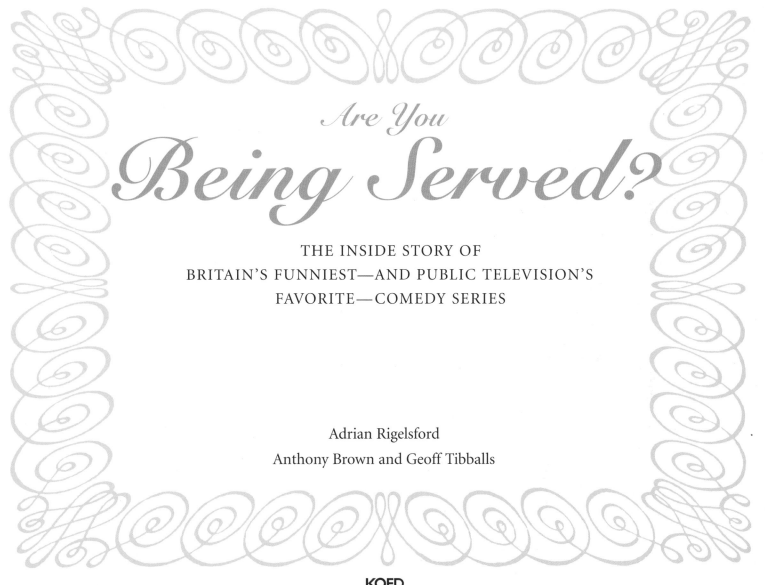

Are You Being Served?

THE INSIDE STORY OF BRITAIN'S FUNNIEST—AND PUBLIC TELEVISION'S FAVORITE—COMEDY SERIES

Adrian Rigelsford

Anthony Brown and Geoff Tibballs

KQED
BOOKS

SAN FRANCISCO

For information, address :
KQED Books & Tapes,
2601 Mariposa St., San Francisco, CA 94110.

VICE PRESIDENT FOR PUBLISHING & NEW VENTURES:
Mark K. Powelson

PUBLISHER: Pamela Byers
PROJECT EDITOR: Karen Sharpe
PROJECT CO-ORDINATOR FOR U.K.: Simon Carter
RESEARCH ASSISTANT: Ellen Baskin
BOOK DESIGN: Raul Cabra
COVER DESIGN: Louise Kollenbaum
PRINTING SERVICES: Penn&Ink/Hong Kong

KQED PRESIDENT & CEO:
Mary G. F. Bitterman

Photographs © Luke Books Ltd.
and Lumiere Pictures and used by permission.

Permission to reproduce the *Are You Being Served?*
theater poster and book cover courtesy of Jeremy Lloyd.

Excerpts from the *Are You Being Served?*
Fan Club Newsletter
© Marcia Richards and used by permission.

Educational and non-profit groups wishing to order
this book at attractive quantity discounts may contact
KQED Books & Tapes, 2601 Mariposa St.,
San Francisco, CA 94110.

LIBRARY OF CONGRESS CATALOGING-IN-PUBLICATION DATA

RIGELSFORD, ADRIAN, 1966–
   Are you being served? : the inside story of
Britain's funniest — and Public Television's
favorite — comedy series / Adrian Rigelsford,
Anthony Brown & Geoff Tibballs.
     p.   cm.
   Filmography: p.
   ISBN 0-912333-04-9
   1. Are you being served? (Television
program) I. Brown, Anthony, 1967-   .
II. Tibballs, Geoff. III. Title.
PN1992.77.A78R54 1995
791.45'72—dc20   95-1623
                                           CIP

ISBN 0-912333-04-9

10 9 8 7 6 5 4 3 2

ON THE COVER:
John Inman as Mr. Humphries

Distributed to the trade by Publishers Group West

Directory

ACKNOWLEDGMENTS

With special thanks to Gary, Sharon, and Luke Shoefield.

We would also like to thank Trevor Bannister for his time; John Baylis (from Simpson's); Alexandra Cann (Jeremy Lloyd's agent); and Vivien Clore (David Croft's agent); Andy Davidson for his research assistance; John S. Hall for his comments on *Beanes of Boston*; *Laugh* magazine for information about the *Are You Being Served?* Australian series; Paul Laurance (UK legal consultant); Steven Moffat for his introductions; Bob Spiers for taking the time to be interviewed; and David Croft.

On the American side, we wish to thank KQED Books and Mark Powelson and Pamela Byers for believing in the project; Karen Sharpe for shaping and directing it; Ellen Baskin for filling in the information gaps; and Raul Cabra for capturing the right visual sensibility. Candace Carlisle of BBC Worldwide Americas provided important access to information. Our thanks, also, to Catherine Hoffman, Kim Haglund, Martin Venezky, Laura Ferguson, Cesar Rubio, Maxine Ressler, Suzanne Scott, Barbara Ferenstein, and Papi.

We are also grateful to Cathy Lykes, Director of Program Underwriting for PBS, James Scalem, PBS Vice President for Fundraising Programming, and Kevin Harris, KQED-TV Station Manager, whose enthusiastic early support helped bring this project into being.

For Gill Amos, because I always said I'd dedicate the first one to her.
—Anthony Brown

Foreword

THE BASIS OF ALL GOOD COMEDY IS A REALISTIC substructure on which fantasy can be played, and *Are You Being Served?* is definitely grounded in reality. While working at Simpson's department store for more than two years (before being 𝔤𝔦𝔳𝔢𝔫 𝔱𝔥𝔢 𝔟𝔬𝔬𝔱 for selling drinks in a fitting room at the height of a heat wave), I managed to ingest the atmosphere of what would have been described then as an emporium—a place where old-world manners were encouraged and a pecking order was strictly adhered to.

The characters in the cast were an exaggeration of real people I had met there and at other places, and that's what made them so easy to write. The ex-captain patrolling the gentlemen's outfitting floor in Simpson's often pointed to me and asked, "Are you free?" I immediately shot an immaculate cuff, gave a discreet cough, and nodded, hoping to make a sale (and get my 5 percent commission). A lot of Mrs. Slocombe's expressions were used by my grandmother, who came from the north. Miss Brahms is like typical girls of her time: great figures, lots of lipstick, high heels, looking for love but thinking they're too good for most men they meet—and being right in that. Girls like Miss Brahms still exist in small towns and villages throughout Britain, although their accents may vary. The military background for Captain Peacock came from cowriter and producer David Croft, who had had an exciting career as a major in the Far East. Both of us had acting backgrounds, so we knew how shop girls and landladies talked. And we were sufficiently acquainted with people in the upper echelons of society to be able to add a bit of high-class dialogue when required.

Are You Being Served? may not be politically correct, but it's politically accurate, as it stems from our experiences in real life. Unknown to me at the time

(to) 𝔤𝔦𝔳𝔢 𝔱𝔥𝔢 𝔟𝔬𝔬𝔱
to fire from a job

I wrote the series, introducing a character with the camp attitude Mr. Humphries displayed was considered politically incorrect. Yet in our theater days, David and I had known many such characters who were charming, amusing, and much loved—like Mr. Humphries.

What is so appealing about the characters of *Are You Being Served?* is that they are like a family. Mr. Grainger is a rather gruff but kindly grandfather figure. Captain Peacock is like a wicked uncle, and Mrs. Slocombe is like the dotty aunt who 𝔠𝔞𝔩𝔩𝔰 𝔯𝔬𝔲𝔫𝔡, dropping her aitches while being frightfully grand. Mr. Lucas is, at the beginning of the series, the voice of reason in modern-day Britain (as it was then), making fun of the old-fashioned values and practices, not to mention the pecking order. And, of course, everyone would like to have such a friend as Mr. Humphries, who is great fun to be with; any dinner party he attends is guaranteed to be a success.

It is often adversity that draws our little family together, whether it be Mr. Rumbold's pomposity, which they all do their best to unseat, or some outside fate that could overtake the store and put them all out of their jobs. Even the maintenance men, Mr. Mash and Mr. Harman, who represent the underclass, join with the family in times of emergency.

The characters engender much sympathy from the audience, and that also adds to their appeal. Captain Peacock represents every middle-management person nearing retirement age, trying to keep his dignity and wondering how he is going to afford his retirement. I always feel a great sympathy for him because I'm facing the same problems myself. I also feel much sympathy for Miss Brahms. She's stuck in the sort of job in which one can't move up to the next position until the person above dies—and Mrs. Slocombe looks very robust. Miss Brahms' salary is not very good, she has to look her best all day, and she must be polite to people, many of whom are extremely rude. I can easily empathize

(to) 𝔠𝔞𝔩𝔩 𝔯𝔬𝔲𝔫𝔡
pay a visit, drop over

with her because I, too, have experienced that rudeness shown so often to people who are providing a service.

As the characters develop, the audience comes to know them better and to regard them as old friends. Aware of their idiosyncrasies, the audience can guess what the characters' reactions to most situations will be, and is rarely disappointed. What draws the audience in is the characters' ability to attack and defend verbally in an amusing way while they attempt to cope with situations as they come along. The audience pays no great attention to the plot so long as the tension between the characters is sustained by their individuality.

Today, more than 20 years after we began the series, the world is a very different place. While *Are You Being Served?* may seem a little old-fashioned, nothing, to paraphrase Noel Coward, is as old-fashioned as something that's supposed to be totally modern, and nothing is so totally modern as something that was once considered old-fashioned. I think that's why *Are You Being Served?* is such a world-wide success: It's suddenly totally modern, and it shows a world to which we'd all like to return.

BY ADRIAN RIGELSFORD

Introduction

THE COMEDY ROOTS OF *ARE YOU BEING SERVED?* stretch back some ten years before the series began. Until the fall of 1955, the BBC had dominated television's airwaves in England for the simple reason that no competition existed. That September, however, Independent Television (ITV) started broadcasting, and the BBC suddenly found it had to compete against ITV for the relatively small number of viewers. Situation comedies quickly became a staple part of the programming diet, and the BBC won hands down on that front for the rest of the decade. This success was largely due to Tony Hancock.

Hancock belonged to the generation of comedians who had learned their trade at the famous Windmill Theatre in London in the late 1940s. The shows there consisted of "Still Lifes," in which naked showgirls held poses for several minutes against backgrounds that parodied famous paintings, such as the *Mona Lisa* (with the showgirl wearing nothing but her enigmatic smile). It was up to the comedians to keep the audiences entertained while the sets were changed.

Within a year of beginning his own radio series in 1954, Hancock had become a national institution. He quickly made the transition to television with *Hancock's Half Hour.* This comedy show was effectively the first British sitcom, with the cast playing the same characters from week to week and each show having a plot. *Hancock's Half Hour* could quite literally clear the streets whenever an episode aired. Over the course of six seasons, Hancock worked with consistently inventive scripts by Ray Galton and Alan Simpson. But after ten years of working together, Galton and Simpson parted company with the increasingly troubled Hancock, who eventually took his life.

By the beginning of 1962, Galton and Simpson wanted to explore new areas of comedy writing and to develop new projects. The BBC was just as keen not to lose them to ITV, which had yet to equal the BBC's track record with comedy. *Comedy Playhouse* was devised as a means for the two writers to create whatever kind of sitcom they wanted. The six half-hour shows were intended as playlets more than anything else. If one proved especially successful, it could always be turned into a series. And that is, in fact, what happened to a number of episodes, generally one a season. *Steptoe and Son* (*Sanford and Son* in the US) and *Till Death Us Do Part* (*All in the Family* in the US) came out of *Comedy Playhouse*, as did the 1968 hit *Dad's Army*, set in England during the Second World War. David Croft and Jimmy Perry cowrote the scripts for *Dad's Army*, and went on to create such other hits as *It Ain't Half Hot, Mum*, *Hi-de-Hi!*, and *'Allo, 'Allo*. Croft was an experienced comedy producer at the BBC, but *Dad's Army* was one of the first shows for which he had assumed full creative control from conception to broadcast.

Toward the end of 1971, a new batch of scripts was being commissioned for the upcoming year. To be accepted for consideration, submissions had to conform to two basic guidelines: They had to have little, if any, requirements for location filming; and the central action of the plot had to revolve around one main studio set, with up to three "sub" or minor sets.

At that time, Jeremy Lloyd was working as both a writer and an actor. He had devised what seemed to be an ideal setup for a situation comedy, and the easiest way to test its viability—and ultimately the reaction of the viewers—was to have it broadcast as part of *Comedy Playhouse*. So Lloyd approached producer Croft with his idea and won a commission to write the pilot script. The basic story revolved around the exploits of shop assistants working in the clothing section of a vast department store. The result was *Are You Being Served?*, the amazing history of which fills the following pages.

Filmography

BBC TV, 1972–1985, 69 EPISODES

written by
**JEREMY LLOYD AND
DAVID CROFT**
(and Michael Knowles, four episodes)

produced by
**DAVID CROFT
HAROLD SNOAD** · *1974*

BOB SPIERS · *1983*

MARTIN SHARDLOW · *1975*

MIKE STEVENS · *1992-1993*

directed by
**DAVID CROFT
HAROLD SNOAD** · *1974*

RAY BUTT · *1975-1977*

BOB SPIERS · *1977-1978, 1983*

GORDON ELSBURY · *1979*

JOHN KILBY · *1981*

MARTIN SHARDLOW · *1985*

MIKE STEVENS · *1992-1993*

starring
JOHN INMAN
as Mr. Humphries · *1972-1985*

MOLLIE SUGDEN
as Mrs. Slocombe · *1972-1985*

WENDY RICHARD
as Miss Brahms · *1972-1985*

FRANK THORNTON
as Captain Peacock · *1972-1985*

TREVOR BANNISTER
as Mr. Lucas · *1972-1979*

NICHOLAS SMITH
as Mr. Rumbold · *1972-1985*

ARTHUR BROUGH
as Mr. Grainger · *1972-1977*

HAROLD BENNETT
as Young Mr. Grace · *1972-1981*

ARTHUR ENGLISH
as Mr. Harman · *1976-1985*

MIKE BERRY
as Mr. Spooner · *1981-1985*

LARRY MARTYN
as Mr. Mash · *1972-1975*

ALFIE BASS
as Mr. Goldberg · *1979*

KENNETH WALLER
as Old Mr. Grace · *1981*

JAMES HAYTER
as Mr. Tebbs · *1978*

MILO SPERBER
as Mr. Grossman · *1981*

BENNY LEE
as Mr. Klein · *1981*

with
Stephanie Gathercole
as the Secretary · *1972-1973*

Penny Irving
as Miss Bakewell · *1976-1979*

Vivienne Johnson
as the Nurse · *1978-1981*

Debbie Linden
as the Secretary · *1981*

Candy Davis
as Miss Belfridge · *1983-1985*

Doremy Vernon
as the Canteen Manageress · *1975-1985*

3

CHAPTER 1

GRACE BROS.

THE *Cast*

OF CHARACTERS

GRACE
BROS.

BOARD OF DIRECTORS:
Jeremy Lloyd
David Croft

FULL-TIME STAFF:

Mr. Wilberforce Clayborne Humphries
Sales Assistant in Gentlemen's Ready-to-Wear

Mrs. Betty Slocombe
Senior Saleswoman in Ladies' Separates and Underwear

Miss Shirley Brahms
Assistant Saleswoman in Ladies' Separates and Underwear

Captain Stephen Peacock
Floorwalker

Mr. James (or Dick) Lucas
Junior Salesman in Gentlemen's Ready-to-Wear

Mr. Cuthbert Rumbold
Store Manager

Mr. Ernest Grainger
Senior Salesman in Gentlemen's Ready-to-Wear

Young Mr. Grace
Store Owner

Mr. Beverley Harman
Maintenance Man/Porter

PART-TIME STAFF:

Mr. Bert Spooner
Junior Salesman in Gentlemen's Ready-to-Wear

Mr. Percival Tebbs
Senior Salesman in Gentlemen's Ready-to-Wear

Mr. Harry Goldberg
Senior Salesman in Gentlemen's Ready-to-Wear

Mr. Mash
Maintenance Man/Porter

Old Mr. Grace
Store Owner

CASTING THE
Characters

MUCH OF THE SUCCESS OF *ARE YOU BEING SERVED?* rests with the characters and the actors playing them. Plot is generally secondary to the interaction among the Grace Brothers staff and the revelation of their idiosyncrasies, their quirks, their conflicts, and their likes and dislikes (which, in the case of Mrs. Slocombe, are many).

In assembling the actors, David Croft called upon the services of two actresses he had cast previously in *Dad's Army*—Mollie Sugden and Wendy Richard—for the parts of Mrs. Slocombe and Miss Brahms, respectively. Croft found in Frank Thornton, whom he cast as Captain Peacock, an actor with a wealth of experience in television comedy. Thornton's career stretched back more than ten years to his work with Tony Hancock, who was effectively the founder of the British sitcom. Giving the part of Mr. Lucas to Trevor Bannister brought another familiar face to the show (Bannister was well known for his work on *The Dustbinmen*, which enjoyed an extraordinary success during its initial broadcast in the late 1960s).

After choosing Nicholas Smith, Harold Bennett, Larry Martyn, and Arthur Brough, Croft gave the role of Mr. Humphries to John Inman, who, up until that point, was relatively unknown, although he had extensive stage experience to his credit.

As an ensemble, the entire group worked together with exceptional ease right from the initial rehearsals for the pilot, with Inman, Thornton, Richard, Sugden, and Smith staying together for the course of the series' eleven-year run and then reuniting in 1992 for the spin-off series **Grace and Favour** (called *Are You Being Served? Again!* in the United States), which lasted for two seasons.

There's a saying that "A cast that stays together plays together," and that's certainly true of many of the *Are You Being Served?* actors, who openly admit that lifelong friendships were formed on the Grace Brothers floor, and these have endured to the present.

dustbinman
garbage collector, also dustman

grace and favour
an expression used in connection with a piece of property (such as an apartment or small cottage) and referring to rent-free occupancy awarded to a retired loyal retainer, royal or otherwise

"It takes a strange breed of actor to survive the rigors of the world of the situation comedy. They have to possess that unique spirit which so many music hall comedians had, and have the ability to stand there in the face of all adversity and work the material until they finally get a laugh. Unlike the music hall, they face a far harder audience—the viewing audience who, like Nero, just has to give the thumbs down and switch off the television to kill them off." —a commentator

Keeping Order at Grace Brothers

There is a clear hierarchical structure that organizes the Grace Brothers staff, an order that they all respect, with a division between management and staff. The division is emphasized by the key to the executive washroom, which the staff hope one day to receive. The order carried over even into the canteen, as can be seen in the table placings, where Captain Peacock was at the head with the seniors on either side of him, and the lesser people further down the table.

If you start at the top, Mr. Rumbold represents the management, which is constantly trying to keep control but is very unimaginative and finds it very hard to cope with situations. Under him is Captain Peacock, who retains his rank of captain in the army even though he was only in the catering corps. He's someone who actually existed in the stores while I was working in them, who had to wear his regimental tie with a nice handkerchief in his top pocket so as to assert his authority and keep control between the counters. Beneath him is the men's counter, and the head of the men's counter is Mr. Grainger, an old-time assistant—fussy and pedantic, but charming. Beneath him is Mr. Humphries, and how can I describe him? He's an enthusiastic innocent, a bit of a mother's boy, who has beneath him Mr. Lucas, who was the third assistant on the counter, the boy (even though he was a bit old to be a boy). Again, there was a pecking order amongst them. Mr. Grainger got the first go at each customer who came in, Mr. Humphries would get the second customer, and then the boy would get the third, except that if the third looked as if he was rich and was going to spend a lot, then the head salesman would take over. The boy just couldn't win!

Over on the ladies' counter, Mrs. Slocombe is something of a mother figure, just as Mr. Grainger is a grandfather figure. She is a matronly figure with a young daughter-like assistant. The younger the assistants were, the more disruptive they were; the young ones would not go along with the order all the time, and would have to be pulled into line.

Then there was the cleaner, Mr. Mash, who worked in the cellar and was a sort of Bolshevik really; he knew his position in the store but resented it. Everybody with a better job felt better than everyone else, so they all felt better than he. The canteen manageress was also of the lower order, and could easily be upset, so she went on strike and disrupted the ordered structures.

Another way to look at it is that the Grace Brothers staff is a family, with Captain Peacock as the head of the family, Mr. Grainger as the grandfather, and Young Mr. Grace as the family patriarch.

—*Jeremy Lloyd*

THE PRANK THAT GOT JEREMY LLOYD HIS big break in the TV world is one that would make anyone applying for a job at Grace Brothers applaud with due admiration. One day in 1969, while sitting in the London office of his agent, Lloyd answered the phone and found himself talking to George Schlatter, producer of *Rowan and Martin's Laugh-In*. Schlatter wanted to know whether the organization had any talent who could come to America and write for the show.

"Yes," answered Lloyd eagerly. "We've got Jeremy Lloyd. He's our best writer. He writes for the top comedy shows here. He's expensive, but he's good."

Schlatter met Lloyd at the Dorchester Hotel the following morning. Lloyd performed some of his sketches, and Schlatter announced that he was teaming him up with Arte Johnson's twin brother, Coslough, who was little more than 5 feet tall (Lloyd is 6 feet 4 inches). "We'll all get a laugh when you guys walk down the corridor together," exclaimed Schlatter.

From Sickly Child to
Suit Salesman at Simpson's

Lloyd's route to fame had not been nearly so serendipitous as his *Laugh-In* coup. He grew up a lonely, sickly child. His mother, one of the dancing Tiller Girls, left home when he was barely a year old, and his father, a lieutenant-colonel in the army, dispatched young Jeremy to a Cheshire boarding school where the main use for books was protecting tender backsides from the cane.

At the end of the Second World War, Lloyd's father found him a job as a plumber's apprentice. "I was a good plumber's **mate**," he recalls, "because I was so thin. They could give me the jobs that involved crawling inside boilers." But plumbing made him ill, and so his father got him a job in a Hertfordshire metal foundry. That made him even more ill.

mate
an assistant or apprentice; also, a good friend

By 21, the only thing Lloyd did know was that whatever profession he tried next, it would not be chosen by his father. This decision led him to the position of suit salesman at Simpson's in London's Piccadilly. There he observed the pecking order among the staff of the Gentlemen's Ready-to-Wear Department and picked up such phrases as "I'm free" and "Are you being served?" These were to serve him extraordinarily well some 20 years later.

"It was an amazing place," he says. "I used to watch the senior assistant assessing the customer's spending power. If it didn't look very good, he'd be passed on with a nod to the second senior assistant and maybe further on down the line. I was the junior. I would only get people who came in with holes in their shoes."

Lloyd didn't stay long at Simpson's, his departure having been hastened when he was caught selling soft drinks in the menswear department. But he never forgot his experiences at the store.

Lloyd's next job was in the glamourous world of industrial paint. As he whiled away another sale-less afternoon in the cinema, he

"Recently I was invited to lunch by Her Majesty the Queen Mother and Princess Margaret, as they are both great fans of Are You Being Served? and 'Allo, 'Allo. It occurred to me as the liveried servants served lunch that as a writer you constantly live in a world of imagination, and that this seemed to be an extension of it. Had I been Mr. Humphries, I would probably have told the Queen Mother that the first time I remember seeing her with her daughters was a picture on top of a cake tin. I didn't slip into Mr. Humphries' mode, though I was very tempted."
—Jeremy Lloyd

decided to write a screenplay about the Loch Ness Monster called *What a Whopper.* It was bought by Pinewood Film Studios, and the resulting production starred British pop singer Adam Faith. Suitably inspired, Lloyd went on to write and appear in one of the BBC's first pop-music shows, *Six-Five Special,* before putting his large frame to good use as an upper-class twit in the long-running *Billy Cotton Bandshow.*

twit
a jerk

The *Laugh-In* gig came nearly ten years later. "It was an exhausting business, writing and appearing in [the show]. Often recording sessions would go on until three in the morning," Lloyd recalls. He soon realized that Hollywood was not all glamour, a fact brought home to him when he was turned down for the part of a string bean in a vegetable soup commercial.

In 1970, back in England on a break from *Laugh-In,* Lloyd married actress Joanna Lumley. They split up four months later.

Itching to Do a Sitcom

Having found success in show business as a writer and performer, Lloyd wanted to write a situation comedy. "I came up with this idea about life in a department store, based loosely on my memories of Simpson's," he explains. "I offered the idea to Lew Grade's ATV, but they said it wasn't the sort of thing they did."

He also sent a copy to BBC producer David Croft, whom he had met briefly while working on a comedy series called *It's Awfully Bad for Your Eyes, Darling.* At the time, Croft was cowriting and producing *Dad's Army,* a series about the English Home Guard during World War Two, which went on to become one of Britain's most popular and enduring comedies. Croft liked the department store idea, and *Are You Being Served?* was born. "It was tremendous fun to do," says Lloyd.

Jeremy Lloyd's most frightening moment on Laugh-In was when Danny Kaye, standing with a lamp shade on his head, pretending to be a demented U-boat commander, took a sudden dislike to the script and demanded to know who had written it. Terrified to admit responsibility, Lloyd joined Kaye in his tantrum and blamed two other writers.

With Are You Being Served? at its height, Lloyd enjoyed parallel success with a children's book of poems titled Captain Beaky and His Band. ("Beaky" had been one of Lloyd's more repeatable nicknames at school.)

In 1978, Lloyd collaborated again with David Croft on the comedy series *Oh, Happy Band!*, starring the bumbling Harry Worth. The partnership enjoyed a much greater triumph in 1984 with *'Allo, 'Allo.*

"David and I were hammering out an idea for a sitcom which wasn't really working, " Lloyd explains. "I racked my brains to think of an alternative. To me, the most important thing in comedy is the setting. You have to have a set which remains constant so that lots of people can come and go and do their thing, say their bit, and go away again. It seemed to me that a clandestine French farce set in a café during the war would provide this."

This idea came to Lloyd sometime after midnight. "David always goes to bed at 11 p.m., but I phoned and woke him up and said, 'Could we not abandon what we're doing and try a French Resistance comedy?' He said, 'We'll start in the morning,' put the phone down, and that was *'Allo, 'Allo.*"

A keen racing driver, Lloyd recently married lion tamer Collette Northrop, who brought a wild panther to their wedding at Palm Beach. He was even more recently divorced. Collette has returned to a quiet life with wild animals, Lloyd to his writing desk. He remains a lovable English eccentric.

"Looking back, I find my life hysterically funny. Even if I sometimes feel really wretched, I look in the mirror and roar with laughter at the sight of my own downcast reflection, and think about writing a new show and making friends with the characters who lurk somewhere deep in my mind waiting to run down my arm and onto the blank white pages." —Jeremy Lloyd

Career
HIGHLIGHTS

TV CREDITS INCLUDE
Six-Five Special (actor)

Billy Cotton Bandshow (actor)

150 scripts for The Dickie Henderson Show (writer)

Rowan and Martin's Laugh-In (actor, writer)

Oh, Happy Band! (cowriter with David Croft)

'Allo, 'Allo (cowriter with David Croft)

Come Back, Mrs. Noah (cowriter with David Croft)

Grace and Favour (actor and cowriter)

FILM CREDITS INCLUDE
We Joined the Navy (actor)

A Very Important Person (actor)

Those Magnificent Men in Their Flying Machines (actor)

The Wrong Box (actor)

Doctor in Clover (actor)

The Bawdy Adventures of Tom Jones (writer)

Are You Being Served? (writer)

Vampira (writer)

THEATER CREDITS INCLUDE
Are You Being Served? (writer)

DAVID
Croft

FOR NEARLY 30 YEARS, DAVID CROFT HAS been the King Midas of television comedy, whether as cowriter, producer, or director; everything he has touched has turned to gold. This good fortune began in 1968 with *Dad's Army,* which ran for 80 episodes, and continued with *Are You Being Served?* Next came *It Ain't Half Hot, Mum* (1974), the tales of a platoon of British solders organizing a **concert party** in India during the war. That series ran for 56 episodes.

In 1981 came the first of 58 episodes of *Hi-de-Hi!,* a **pantomime**-style lark about the staff of a 1950s holiday camp, followed in 1984 by *'Allo, 'Allo,* which ran for nine years. More recently, Croft came up with *You Rang, M'Lord?,* a spoof on *Upstairs Downstairs,* the long-running saga about life in an aristocratic English household in the early years of this century.

concert party
a group of traveling soldiers—actors before conscription—who put on musical and comedy performances for troops

pantomime
a show produced during the Christmas season, usually based on fairy tales or ancient legends, which incorporates singing, dancing, and, most notably, very broad humor

Croft is the master of "gang-show" comedy (*Are You Being Served?* falls in this genre), a style in which a large cast of regular characters performs on a limited number of sets. The characters are finely drawn, each with their own idiosyncrasies and, invariably, unique catchphrases. The viewer knows what a given character is going to say each week in a certain situation, though this in no way detracts from the viewer's enjoyment. On the contrary, part of the success of Croft's scripts derives from the audience's familiarity with the characters, with its being able to anticipate the dialogue. With these sorts of expectations, the omission of a favorite catchphrase could lead to disappointment. In gang-show comedies, familiarity breeds content.

Croft opts for familiarity in choosing his actors, too. He tends to cast those he has worked with previously. Very often, an actor with only a minor role in one Croft series will be promoted to stardom in the next. Of the *Are You Being Served?* cast, Wendy Richard, Harold Bennett, Arthur Brough, and Larry Martyn all had had cameo roles in *Dad's Army*. Gorden Kaye had a minor part in *Are You Being Served?* before going on to star in *'Allo, 'Allo*. Paul Shane, Su Pollard, and Jeffrey Holland all had leading roles in *Hi-de-Hi!* and *You Rang, M'Lord?*, and Michael Knowles and Donald Hewlett had leading roles in *It Ain't Half Hot, Mum* and *You Rang, M'Lord?* Bill Pertwee was in *Dad's Army* and *You Rang, M'Lord?* The connections are endless.

"Doing a television series is no different from any other walk of life," says Croft. "It's nice to work with people you know. Also, because you've worked with them in the past, you know that they are going to produce the goods. It's a feeling of mutual trust."

While his actor parents were appearing at London's Hippodrome Theater, baby David slept in a prop basket. Their dressing room served as his nursery. At the age of four, he caused a commotion by accidentally wandering onto the stage at the Shaftesbury Theatre in London, where his parents were playing.

David Croft hails from a theatrical background. His parents, Anne Croft and Reginald Sharland, were big stars of the twenties and thirties. With such an upbringing, it was inevitable that young David would follow in his parents' footsteps, and so, in 1938, he made his film debut as a butcher's boy in *Goodbye Mr. Chips,* starring Robert Donat.

After the war, he appeared in countless stage productions and, as a lyricist, collaborated with musician Cyril Ornadel on a number of shows at the London Palladium. For a while, Croft sang with the BBC Show Band Singers, backing many international stars on radio and record, before turning his attention to television. It was as a writer and director at Tyne-Tees TV, in the northeast of England, that he first worked with Mollie Sugden. When he later moved to the BBC as a director, working on the popular comedy series *Hugh and I,* which starred Terry Scott and Hugh Lloyd, he again cast Sugden, this time as a snooty neighbor. Nearly ten years later, he knew once more that she would be absolutely right for the part of Mrs. Slocombe in *Are You Being Served?*

David Croft, **OBE**, is justifiably proud of his prolific output and has many fond memories. "The thing about working with Jeremy—and this was true on both *Are You Being Served?* and *'Allo, 'Allo*—is that when we're together we laugh a lot. Of course we're disciplined writers, but we do also like to enjoy ourselves."

Indeed, when Croft suffered a heart attack during production of *Are You Being Served?* and Jeremy Lloyd went to visit him in the hospital, Lloyd had to be asked to leave because he was making the patient laugh so much.

OBE
Order of the British Empire; one of the honorary titles given to a British subject and awarded on the monarch's birthday, on New Year's Day, or at the time of a prime minister's resignation

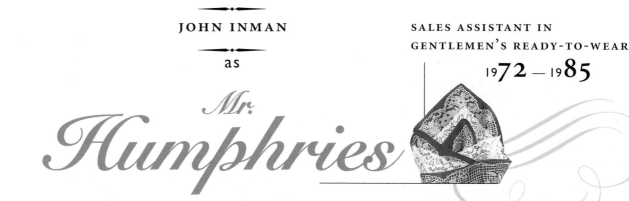

JOHN INMAN

as

SALES ASSISTANT IN
GENTLEMEN'S READY-TO-WEAR

19**72** — 19**85**

Mr. *Humphries*

WITH HIS MINCING WALK, LIKE A BALLERINA WALKING ON hot coals, and a voice so trill that often only dogs can hear it, Wilberforce Clayborne Humphries has happily dedicated his life to measuring inside legs. As the assistant in Gentlemen's Ready-to-Wear, he has become an expert salesman who knows all the tricks of the trade. He **knees** jackets, and if trousers are too tight, he goes away and returns with the same pair, telling the customer that it's a larger size. It never fails. On one occasion, he grips first the front and then the back of a doubting customer's too-loose jacket to make it fit better.

Warm and affectionate and more precious than the Crown Jewels, Mr. Humphries always gives the impression that he is pleased to see everyone. He lives with his mother, who rides a motorcycle and sidecar combination. If he is not home by one o'clock in the morning, she locks him out. The family theatrical background made him a natural to train the Grace Brothers' team for the inter-store ballroom dancing competition in the episode "Top Hat and Tails." Mr. Humphries resents the assumption that all his friends are men and goes to great lengths (something he is always eager to do) to give examples of his female friends. But in the *Are You Being Served?* film, he comments that his three gorgeous female companions confess that they're much happier since they've had the "change."

mincing
dainty, only affectedly so

(to) knee
a fitting technique whereby a tight garment is made roomier by breaking some stitches by stretching it across a knee

Mr. Humphries was a founding member of the British Union of Mackintosh and Overcoat Factors and Fitters

(BUMOFF)

John Inman's interpretation of Mr. Humphries is based on the shop assistants he worked with during a brief stint as a window dresser at the Austin Reed store in London's Regent Street—not too far from Simpson's.

"It was funny," says Inman. "One day we were rehearsing *Are You Being Served?* and Mollie Sugden came in, having been shopping at a smart gents' outfitters that morning. The man behind the counter had recognized her and said, 'I know John Inman, you know. I trained with him in menswear. Pass on my best wishes.'

"When she arrived at rehearsal, she told me the story and asked, 'Do you remember him?'

"'Remember him?' I laughed. 'I got the walk from him!'"

Inman will never forget the moment that Mr. Humphries minced into his life. "I was in a Christmas show and was also doing a spot of toy selling at Selfridge's, the big London store. A friend came in and said David Croft wanted me to work with him. I walked out of Selfridge's and never went back."

That was more than 20 years ago, and Inman still relishes the role. "Mr. Humphries has been very good to me. I always get a real kick out of playing him. He makes remarks that I wouldn't dare say in real life. Mind you, he is never easy to play. It would be easy to go over the top and spoil it altogether.

"There came a point in the show when the lines got more and more outrageous, and David Croft would say, 'Dare we do that?'

"I said, 'David, you have created a monster. You have to let him go.'"

Most British viewers automatically concluded that Mr. Humphries was gay, but Inman refutes the suggestion. "It has never been mentioned one way or the other," he argues. "So whenever

mackintosh or mac
raincoat

people talk to me about Mr. Humphries being gay, I say that until you see him do it over the counter, how do you know? He's just a bit precious, he's got a wicked tongue, and he lives with his mother. But many people do. He makes a very nice Yorkshire pudding and he likes to go out to parties. But I think he's as wide-eyed about the whole thing as anybody."

Inman never ceases to be amazed by the reaction he gets to Mr. Humphries. The shouts of "Are you free?" from fans has never stopped. "When the show first started, I couldn't pass a school playground without hearing the calls. Now I have difficulty passing a pub. The same kids have reached drinking age, but they haven't forgotten Mr. Humphries. People write to me from all over the world, sending me socks and pullovers and almost every item of clothing you can imagine. I think they all want to mother me."

The only negative reaction to the character Inman has ever gotten came from Britain's gay community—and even then the occasions were isolated. "One or two people did think I was playing a stereotype gay person, but I don't really understand what they meant. If you play a stereotype 𝔩𝔬𝔯𝔯𝔶 driver, you wear big boots and jeans. Does that mean because you wear a neat little suit and a tie you must be gay?"

General Dogsbody to "Funniest Man on Television"

Born in Preston, on June 28, 1935, Inman first declared his intention to become an actor at the age of three. At 13, he made his stage debut in a play called *Freda* at the South Pier Pavilion, Blackpool, and two years later, on leaving school, landed a job at the same theater as a general 𝔡𝔬𝔤𝔰𝔟𝔬𝔡𝔶.

𝔠𝔥𝔞𝔱 𝔰𝔥𝔬𝔴𝔰
talk shows

𝔩𝔬𝔯𝔯𝔶
truck

𝔡𝔬𝔤𝔰𝔟𝔬𝔡𝔶
(or 𝔡𝔬𝔤'𝔰 𝔟𝔬𝔡𝔶)
gofer, low person in company hierarchy

Upstaged by War

Inman's first visit to the United States as Mr. Humphries was heavily promoted with a short spot filmed in England saying he was on his way. Eager fans instantly called their local PBS stations to find out details about his visit. His live appearance at KAET in Phoenix was to air at 7 p.m. one evening. But that afternoon, the United States declared war on Iraq and President Bush announced he would address the nation—at 7 p.m. At 6:59 Inman went on the air, saying, "When my friends here in Arizona told me that I'd be coming to speak to you, they told me only one thing would keep me from being on the air—an act of war....So now we present President Bush. But stay tuned—I'll be back." The station raised much money that evening, and Inman signed autographs until his hands were swollen and he literally had to be pulled away.

Career

HIGHLIGHTS

"My problem was that I looked very young for my age. I was never really a juvenile—I was a character actor, and I got to a stage where there wasn't really much work for people who looked like me," Inman explains. "My mother used to say to me, 'John, why don't you get yourself a proper job?' Eventually, I decided to take her advice. That's how I ended up in the shop window of Austin Reed's."

But the lure of the stage proved too powerful. "When I started putting the lights on me and not the mannequin, I thought it was time to leave the world of menswear and go off and do what I really wanted to do—act."

Inman has never looked back. His work has taken him all over the world, and in 1976, he won several awards, including the Variety Club BBC TV Personality of the Year award and the *TV Times* magazine award for Funniest Man on Television.

To many observers, there is little difference between Mr. Humphries and John Inman. Like his character, Inman is often on, slinging one-liners in rapid-fire succession. Pantomime is one of his great loves, and for many years, he and actor Barry Howard made a formidable pair of Ugly Sisters in *Cinderella*. Inman is now established as one of the best pantomime dames in the land.

Although he was engaged when he was 24, Inman has never married. He gets upset when people assume he is as camp as Mr. Humphries. "I'm not the only confirmed bachelor in the world," he says. "The assumption comes because I mince around a counter. In fact, I could quite easily get married, but whoever takes on the job would have to be pretty strong because it wouldn't be the easiest job in the world. I think I'm fairly set in my ways, and my life revolves around my work. The truth is I love show business far more than I could love anything or anyone else."

Although John Inman has always stressed that his camp portrayal of Mr. Humphries was not meant to paint him as being homosexual, the gay community at the time the show first aired was outraged that he reflected the stereotypical image of what gay men were thought to be like.

"Homosexuality was an incredibly taboo subject [when the series was aired]," comments David Walker, a campaigner for gay rights in England since 1969. "When this flamboyant image screamed across the screen, it was like a nail in the coffin of what we were trying to achieve. The majority of people saw gay men as being very waspish, skipping around the place with limp wrists, and that's exactly what they saw on *Are You Being Served?* Of course there were protests, because if you want a large section of the community to be accepted, **sending** them **up** like that does no end of damage."

Phone calls were made to the **duty office** at BBC TV Centre, registering all manner of complaints. Protests were made, and letters were written, demanding that Inman's character be removed from the series. He caused offense and anger in equal portions, and yet it seems the production team pretty much ignored the complaints. Mr. Humphries was popular with the mass audience, who didn't complain, so he stayed on the series.

(to) send up
to make fun of or do a humorous "takeoff" on someone or something

duty office
audience services office

Walker recalls dreading every episode. "I think men of my age [he is in his midfifties], certainly at that time, were just paranoid about what Mr. Humphries would say each week, in case something caught on and something he said could be leveled against us. Looking back on it now, I can't believe how paranoid some sectors were being about the series. It was blown out of proportion completely. I think a lot of people made some serious mistakes in what they were saying. There were petitions demanding that

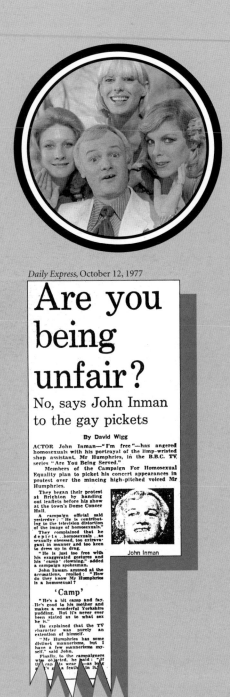

Daily Express, October 12, 1977

Are you being unfair?

No, says John Inman to the gay pickets

By David Wigg

ACTOR John Inman—"I'm free"—has angered homosexuals with his portrayal of the limp-wristed shop assistant, Mr Humphries, in the B.B.C. TV. series "Are You Being Served."

Members of the Campaign For Homosexual Equality plan to picket his concert appearances in protest over the mincing high-pitched voiced Mr Humphries.

They began their protest at Brighton by handing out leaflets before his show at the town's Dome Concert Hall.

A campaign official said yesterday: "He is contributing to the television distortion of the image of homosexuals."

They complained that he depicts . . . homosexuals . . as sexually obsessed, too extravagant in manner and too keen to dress up in drag.

"He is just too free with his exaggerated gestures and his 'camp' clowning," added a campaign spokesman.

John Inman, amused at the accusations, replied: "How do they know Mr Humphries is a homosexual?"

John Inman

'Camp'

"He's a bit camp and fay. He's good to his mother and makes a wonderful Yorkshire pudding. But it's never ever been stated as to what sex he is."

He explained that the TV character was purely an extention of himself.

"Mr Humphries has some distinct mannerisms, but I have a few mannerisms myself," said John.

Finally, to the campaigners who objected, he said: "If they can his wear as long as I've a feather in it."

Inman be sarked from the BBC, and I seem to remember that there was even one group of gay actors who were lobbying for him to be barred from Equity (the actors union) for the rest of his working life, which is ludicrous. It's like the witch hunts.

"The press caught on to this, and there were some headlines that caused a lot of trouble. I remember going to one meeting after the first or maybe the second batch of episodes had been broadcast, and you could have cut the air with a knife. People were genuinely angry that Mr. Humphries had put on women's clothing, or a wig, or something like that, because they immediately felt it reflected on them, the gay society. Yet today, nobody would bat an eyelid. That kind of fear has gone, and that's no bad thing. Thankfully, things are very different now."

Ironically, today Mr. Humphries is regarded by the gay audience as an icon. "He's up there with Judy Garland and Barbra Streisand, worshipped from afar by one and all," says Hanna Rogers, a well-known British feminist poet and a lesbian. "Sure, I think that the series was quite daring for its time. I mean, homosexuality wasn't something that people talked about openly. I'm sure the finger was pointed at the television, with hushed voices saying, 'See that man, he's a ....' But it's a bit different now. So many people who are in the public eye have come out. Gay stars are happy to go on talk shows and say what it's like to be a gay man or a lesbian in today's society. So all the fuss about Mr. Humphries seems a bit lame by today's standards."

"The whole *Are You Being Served?* problem was that Mr. Humphries was more camp than gay, and that made people angry," says Chris Steer, a gay commentator who was too young (only two) to take part in the protests. "Men who were known amongst colleagues as being gay did not want to be tarred with the same brush. It's like thinking, 'He's camp, therefore he must be [gay] as well,' and that's where the heart of the problem was, as far as I can tell."

(to) sack
to fire
(from a job)

"Mr. Humphries, from my point of view, is a wonderful, very theatrical creation, who has the ability to appeal beyond a gay audience," continues Steer. "He's accepted by everyone, and everyone loves him. That's fine, and I'm sure John Inman's all too happy about that fact. Let's be honest—it's given him a hell of a career for the past 20 years, taken him to America and all over the world, and there are not many roles, gay or otherwise, that can do that for an actor."

Jerry Thurrm, a gay fan of the series, sees Mr. Humphries as very different from other gays portrayed in films. "Homosexuals were largely portrayed as being rather predatorial up to that time. Look at *Midnight Cowboy*, with the guy who tries to seduce Jon Voight—he's a genuine madman. And Dirk Bogarde in *The Servant*—he's sinister as hell. Mr. Humphries was an outgoing, friendly extrovert, who was just as easily hurt as everyone else. I know Inman says that the character was not gay, but come on. It's like that old Tom Robinson song, he was 'Glad to Be Gay!'"

Thurrm often invites friends over to watch episodes of *Are You Being Served?* that are aired on some of the cable channels in Britain. "We have 'Mr. Humphries nights.' UK Gold runs the show every Friday night, and some of my friends, both gay and straight, come round and we just sit and watch, and actually near-die laughing. It really is still very funny, and in a way, it's ten times better than most of the stuff that's being made today. Yeah, it's true that John Inman's become a cult figure, but that was inevitable. There's a whole generation out there who grew up watching the show, and now they're coming to terms with what they want from life. If they 'come out,' they look back on *Are You Being Served?* with incredible affection, and that's great."

MOLLIE SUGDEN

as

Mrs. *Slocombe*

SENIOR SALESWOMAN IN
LADIES' SEPARATES
AND UNDERWEAR

1972 — 1985

ALWAYS COY ABOUT HER AGE, MRS. SLOCOMBE ADMITTED TO being 46 in 1976. But that was just the number of men she had tried to **chat up** in that particular week. She is a man-chaser, whose appetite only increased with the departure of her husband 20 years before the series begins. It seems he went out to get some butter and never came back. Not that she feels he was any great loss: Wilting flowers remind her of him.

Mrs. Slocombe had met her husband-to-be during a wartime air raid while she was in the Land Army. She apparently spent much of the war on her back. The German bombs threw her onto her back on Clapham Common during one raid, while the American Air Force did the same on other occasions.

She acquired her rank at Grace Brothers by exercising her charms on Young Mr. Grace many years before the opening episode. At first, she takes a shine to newcomer Mr. Lucas, especially when, in the episode "Dear Sexy Knickers," she intercepts an unaddressed letter from him. Assuming it is meant for her, she concludes that Mr. Lucas must be carrying a torch for her. It emerges later that the letter was intended for Miss Brahms.

Mrs. Slocombe believes that men are becoming more polite—they never try to force themselves on her anymore. She points out that when Mr. Lucas was trapped in the elevator with her, he didn't try anything at all—he just pressed the alarm button and screamed for help.

(to) chat up

to sweet-talk or try to convince someone (usually a member of the opposite sex) of something; to come on to

Mrs. Slocombe's full name is Mrs. Mary Elizabeth (Betty) Jennifer Rachel Yiddell Abergavenny Slocombe. Her maiden name was Yiddell.

33

Mrs. Slocombe's earliest memory is of an uncle with a red face sticking his head into her cot.

"I once saw Are You Being Served? in Jordan—though it is difficult to imagine Arabs laughing at a translation of 'How's your pussy tonight, Mrs. Slocombe?'"
—Mollie Sugden

But she never gives up chasing after men. In the episode "Do You Take This Man?" she seems to have trapped a bouzouki player in a Greek restaurant, only to find that he has a wife back in his native country. Her plight becomes so serious that in "The Erotic Dreams of Mrs. Slocombe," she fantasizes she is romantically entangled with Mr. Humphries.

She has had her beloved cat, Tiddles, since 1969 and has trained it to answer the phone. Captain Peacock takes a keen interest in Mrs. Slocombe's pussy (as her cat is often referred to) amid suggestions that he may have slipped it a saucer of milk in the past.

Mrs. Slocombe's hair undergoes more color changes than a set of traffic lights—from blue to pink to purple in quick-fire succession. But then a girl has to look her best, even if she is now pushing 60—from the wrong direction.

The Inspiration for Mrs. Slocombe

Mollie Sugden reveals that the idea for Mrs. Slocombe's chameleonlike hair was her own. "After we'd done the *Comedy Playhouse* pilot, there was a gap of about a year before we went into the series proper. I started thinking about the character, and it occurred to me that somebody who was as bossy as Mrs. Slocombe would probably have the Hairdressing Department at Grace Brothers right under her thumb. So I suggested to David Croft that Mrs. Slocombe should have different-color hair each week, and he liked the idea," she recalls. "At first, I used to have my own hair done specially for the show, but it meant bleaching it every week and spraying on colored lacquer. Eventually my hair began to suffer, so I started to cheat and wear wigs instead!"

Sugden has known quite a few Mrs. Slocombes in her time. "I've seen plenty of characters like her in real life, complete with the blue rinse and beauty spot," she says. "They just don't recognize

cot
baby's crib

themselves. A childhood friend of mine is now a window dresser for a big store, and she used to tell me all about this awful woman who was a buyer. Part of Mrs. Slocombe is based on that buyer."

So what does Sugden think of Mrs. Slocombe? "She can be a bit of a dragon, but being a shop assistant means she has to remember to bite her tongue. She definitely aspires to greater things and tries to talk frightfully **posh**. But every now and again, the affectation slips because she can't keep it up. And, of course, she will have nothing to do with the likes of Mr. Lucas, whom she considers to be beneath her."

In fact, it was Miss Brahms whom Mr. Lucas wanted to be beneath.

"Captain Peacock is much more to her liking," continues Sugden. "I think in the past, he and Mrs. Slocombe had a bit of a fling, and she still carries a torch for him. They've got something in common in that they both try to be something they're not, to acquire a little social standing. That's why he still refers to himself as 'captain' even though he was only ever a corporal."

In spite of being only too aware of Mrs. Slocombe's faults, Sugden has a soft spot for the old girl. "I've always been very fond of her—she is so vulnerable and silly," she admits. "But she's got absolutely no sense of humor. That is why the most daring of double meanings in the show are delivered deadpan. I must say, sometimes I've got as far as the dress rehearsal before I've realized the double meanings myself!"

Making People Laugh

Mollie Sugden was born in Keighley, Yorkshire, on July 21, 1922. She first experienced the pleasure of making people laugh at the tender age of five. "I had seen a lady recite a funny poem at a Sunday school concert, and I thought to myself, 'I could do that,'"

posh
elegant, first-class, often pretentiously so

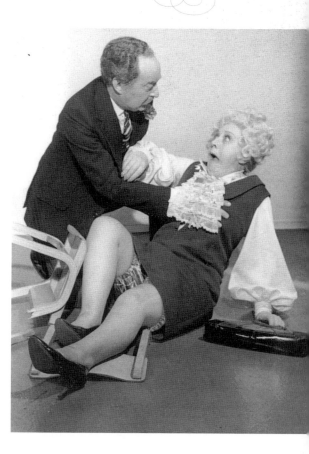

Mrs. Slocombe claims there are two types of underwear: Cold and Interesting, and Warm and Safe.

35

recalls Sugden. "Then at Christmas during a family party, I suddenly got to my feet and announced that I was going to read a poem. My mother said, 'Sit down, don't be so silly.' But I was determined to carry it through. So they stood me on a chair and I did this funny little poem. Everybody was absolutely amazed and roared with laughter, my mother loudest of all. I was thrilled to bits—it was such a lovely feeling making people laugh."

Pursuing an acting career, Sugden traveled to London to join the Guildhall School of Music and Dance. "The first thing they did was iron out my Northern accent and teach me to speak like a duchess. When I left there, I had this frightfully posh accent, but later on, when I started doing North Country comedy with North Country actors, my drama school accent slipped and my true dialect returned. In that respect, Mrs. Slocombe and I are rather alike."

When Sugden graduated to television, she met David Croft, then a trainee director. "David subsequently became a director at the BBC and did a series called *Hugh and I,*" she recalls. "He cast me as a snooty neighbor, the sort with a **steel sink**. She was a marvelous character. Wendy Richard played my niece."

In 1969, Sugden began playing Sandra's ferocious mum, Mrs. Hutchinson, in *The Liver Birds,* a popular BBC comedy about two girls sharing a flat in Liverpool. "Mrs. Hutchinson was a dreadful snob who didn't care about anyone," says Sugden. "I'm glad to say she was nothing like me.

"Not long after, I was doing a **one-off** play and afterward David Croft came round to my dressing room. He said, 'Lovely performance, darling. There's something coming up in the pipeline for you, written especially with you in mind.'

"'Oh,' I said excitedly, 'what is it?' He couldn't tell me at the time, but it turned out to be Mrs. Slocombe."

steel sink
servant's sink, kitchen sink, as distinguished from a porcelain sink, which would be found upstairs in the master's quarters

daft
flighty or silly

one-off
done or performed only once; also, referring to something manufactured, a one-of-a-kind item

Between seasons of *Are You Being Served?* , Sugden starred in a series of her own, *Come Back, Mrs. Noah*, also penned by Croft and Lloyd. "I played a daft, middle-aged housewife in the year 2050 who accidentally went up in a spaceship without a pilot and couldn't get back to Earth," she explains. "It was a nice idea, but, unlike the spaceship, it never really took off."

In 1987, Sugden starred with her real-life husband, William Moore, in the sitcom *My Husband and I.* She met Moore when they were at Swansea Rep together. They married in 1958 and have twin sons, Robin and Simon. "My sons grew up with Mrs. Slocombe, and now my daughters-in-law are having to go through the same thing with *Grace and Favour.*"

Above all, Mollie Sugden cherishes the wonderful camaraderie between the cast members of *Are You Being Served?*

Career

HIGHLIGHTS

TV CREDITS INCLUDE
Hugh and I
Please Sir!
Doctor in the House
For the Love of Ada
The Liver Birds
Coronation Street
Whodunnit?
Come Back, Mrs. Noah
The Tea Ladies
That's My Boy
My Husband and I
Cluedo

FILM CREDITS INCLUDE
Are You Being Served?

THEATER CREDITS INCLUDE
Are You Being Served?

WENDY RICHARD

as

Miss Brahms

ASSISTANT SALESWOMAN
IN LADIES' SEPARATES
AND UNDERWEAR

1972 — 1985

SHIRLEY BRAHMS, MRS. SLOCOMBE'S ASSISTANT, HAS AN OLD head on young shoulders. She is nobody's fool and is adept at getting what she wants from life; if she wants a seat on the bus, she puts her bag under her dress and staggers around, looking pregnant—it always works.

She knows how to handle men, too, particularly Mr. Lucas, whose hands don't just wander—they go off on expeditions. She carries a can opener to deal with just such emergencies and jabs the man in the hand with it if he starts getting too amorous.

To keep body and soul together, she goes out for meals with men she doesn't like: She wears a low-cut frock, her dinner partners have a good look, and she has a good meal. They don't get all that they want, though. She says it's like a **fruit machine**—once they've made the investment, they keep putting in money in the hope that they'll hit the jackpot.

Miss Brahms knows how to keep men interested. Her cleavage, which makes it look as though two Labrador puppies are constantly fighting for attention beneath her dress, is one such way. But if the men get too close, she lashes out with her tongue, which is so sharp she's in danger of lacerating her lips every time she speaks. And there's always the can opener just to make sure the men get the point.

fruit machine
slot machine,
gambling device,
one-armed bandit

Wendy Richard could hardly have made a more spectacular entrance into show business. In 1962, then 15 years old, she teamed up with Mike Sarne to record the novelty song 'Come Outside,' which recounts a lad's increasingly desperate attempts to chat up a girl at a dance. It caught the public's imagination and shot to number one in the British charts, earning Richard the princely sum of £15 in the process.

Richard might not have made much money from the record, but she proved a point to her parents. Born in Middlesbrough in the northeast of England, she lost her native dialect and gained a Cockney accent when she spent eight years helping her mother run a guest house in the King's Cross area of London. "Mum used to complain about my Cockney accent, but I said to her, 'You wait and see—one day I'll make a lot of money out of my voice.' The £15 from "Come Outside" might not have been a fortune, but it turned out to be a stepping stone to greater things."

After completing her general schooling at the Royal Masonic School at Rickmansworth in Hertfordshire, Richard trained at the Italia Conti Stage Academy (England's answer to the School of Performing Arts) and was soon making her name as an actress. Beginning in 1965, she played Cockney teenager Joyce Harker in the BBC soap *The Newcomers* and began to corner the market in such roles. She appeared in two *Carry On* films, *Carry On Matron* and *Carry On Girls,* played bus conductress Doreen in the comedy *On the Buses,* and turned up in numerous other programs, including *The Arthur Haynes Show, Up Pompeii!,* the long-running police series *Z Cars,* and the Secret Service thriller *Danger Man,* which starred Patrick McGoohan. She also came to the notice of David Croft, first in *Hugh and I,* and then as Private Walker's girlfriend in several episodes of *Dad's Army.* So when it came to casting someone to play Miss Brahms in *Are You Being Served?,* Richard was the natural choice.

"I had another qualification for playing Miss Brahms," she says. "After leaving school, I had worked as a shop assistant at the top London stores, Selfridge's and Fortnum and Mason. They were a bit classier than Grace Brothers, but the tips I picked up came in handy nonetheless.

"Miss Brahms is really just an extension of the girl in 'Come Outside'—a bit **sarky**, and someone who likes to give men a run for their money. She might eventually give in to their advances—provided she **fancies** them, of course—but best of all, she enjoys the thrill of the chase. I've loved playing her. She's smashing—always the most sensible of all of them at Grace Brothers. Mind you, that's not saying much."

When *Are You Being Served?* came to an end, Richard was approached for another long-running part, that of Pauline Fowler in the then-new BBC soap *EastEnders*. Julia Smith, the original producer of *EastEnders*, had worked with Wendy on *The Newcomers* and felt that she would be ideal to play frumpy, put-upon Pauline, the woman who could moan for Britain and who seems to have been welded to her cardigan. But Smith was not sure that Richard would be willing to play such a dowdy character after all her younger roles. The answer was simple. "I'm sick of glamour," said Richard. "I want to play my age. It's about time I did."

For the past ten years, Richard has made Pauline one of the best-known characters on British television, with *EastEnders* regularly pulling in audiences of more than 20 million. "It's bloody hard work and far from glamorous," she says. "The worst thing was having my hair cut short after having it long for 19 years. I howled my eyes out, but everyone told me it made me look younger. And at first I was glad to be out of those high heels I used to wear as Miss Brahms. They played havoc with my feet! Mind you, the **washing powder** in the **launderette** where Pauline works used to play hell with my sinuses and gave me a runny nose half the time. I do insist on wearing

sarky
sarcastic

(to) fancy
to like, desire

washing powder
laundry detergent

launderette
laundromat

Apart from being a compulsive giggler, Richard has another major problem: her shortsightedness. "I can only see two feet in front of me. If they move a prop without telling me, I fall over it!"

rubber gloves for 𝔴𝔞𝔰𝔥𝔦𝔫𝔤-𝔲𝔭 scenes, though—just so I can keep my nails nice."

Richard finds that "although Pauline is the salt of the earth, she is a bit dreary, so when I'm away doing other things—like game shows and chat shows—I like to dress up a bit. That's one of the reasons why I was delighted when *Grace and Favour* came up. It was a break from Pauline. I was chomping at the bit to get rid of my cardigan and become miniskirted Miss Brahms again."

Richard had kept in touch with most of the *Are You Being Served?* team anyway, and in 1986, had even recorded a new version of "Come Outside," this time with Mike Berry, who played Mr. Spooner at Grace Brothers.

Sadly, Richard's private life has been less grand than her career. Her father committed suicide when she was only 11, and her first marriage, to Leonard Black, lasted a mere five months. When Richard was 28, her mother died, which devastated her. She then married advertising executive Will Thorpe, but they broke up 18 months later amid lurid headlines in the tabloid press. He spitefully attacked her in print, and she responded by revealing how she had been a battered wife.

She confides that "one day on *Are You Being Served?* I came into work with three lumps on my head where he had hit me and clumps of hair pulled out. I had to have a makeup artist who was good at disguising black eyes."

She is now separated from her third husband, carpetfitter Paul Glorney. "Work has been my salvation so many times when my life has been hell," she says.

In spite of what she has been through, Wendy Richard remains friendly and outgoing. She is the proud owner of a pet cockatiel, Little Henry, and a cairn terrier, Shirley, named after Miss Brahms. She loves tending her patio garden, doing tapestry work, and

𝔴𝔞𝔰𝔥𝔦𝔫𝔤-𝔲𝔭
dishwashing

watching old movies. "I collect clowns and condiment sets, and I'm also an incurable frogophile. I've got a collection of around 400 toy frogs plus frog soap dishes, frog tea pots, and frogs on towels." Miss Brahms would likely hope she could turn one of them into a handsome prince.

FILM CREDITS INCLUDE
Doctor in Clover
No Blade of Grass
Bless This House
On the Buses
Carry On Matron
Gumshoe
Carry On Girls
Are You Being Served?

THEATER CREDITS INCLUDE
No Sex Please—We're British
Let's Go Camping
Blithe Spirit
Are You Being Served?

45

FRANK THORNTON

as

Captain Peacock

FLOORWALKER STEPHEN PEACOCK LIKES EVERYONE TO BELIEVE
that he was a captain in the army and that he served as a desert rat in North
Africa. In truth, he was a mere corporal in the 𝔑𝔞𝔞𝔣𝔦. He also tells people
he was injured in the Suez campaign. He was—he cut himself shaving at
Tilbury Docks.

Captain Peacock lives up to his name, strutting around the floor and paying
constant attention to his plumage. In the very first episode, he instructs Mr.
Lucas on the correct procedure for folding a handkerchief. He places great
store on his status and is delighted when, in "Up Captain Peacock," he
acquires, albeit briefly, a key to the executive toilet and admission to the executive dining room. In "The Hero," in season seven, he feels his authority is
threatened when news seeps out that he has gotten a boil in a particularly
painful spot. He promptly challenges the informant to five rounds in the ring,
but remembers that he is more comfortable in oven gloves than boxing gloves,
and backs down.

He has been married since 1959, but that does not restrain his roving eye.
When Mrs. Peacock was away once, he suggested to Mrs. Slocombe that they
might get together for dinner. She would have accepted had he not also tried
to chat up the girl from the His and Hers perfume company. He shows an
unhealthy interest in the welfare of Mr. Rumbold's secretaries and admires a
girl who is good on the job. In the episode "The Night Club," Miss Belfridge
pulls him toward her in the cinema and calls him "Stephen," implying that this

Naafi

an Armed Forces
canteen, acronym
of Navy, Army, and
Air Force Institutes

(to) call forward

(to) call over

*"Captain Peacock has to have the job of
calling people forward, because otherwise he hasn't got a job. Floorwalker is
a nothing job, but someone greeting
customers when they come in—a
very well dressed man with confidence,
a clicking of the fingers calling over
an assistant, authority—makes the
customer feel good. It also makes the
people "playing the part" feel good:
They might have been very important in
the war, but there's really no place
for them after it, so they have to make
the best of what they've got, and
they place great self-importance
on it."—Jeremy Lloyd*

47

is not the first time they have spent an evening together in the dark. In the episode "Oh What a Tangled Web," from season four, an irate Mrs. Peacock arrives at the store brandishing an umbrella and accuses the Captain of having an affair with another of Mr. Rumbold's secretaries, Miss Hazelwood.

He plays golf (no doubt hoping for a hole-in-one with Mr. Rumbold's secretary), even though his doctor has advised him to give it up because of his bad back. He is no better a golfer than he was a soldier, spending much time in the bunker in both situations.

Captain Peacock has a tattoo of "Death before dishonour" on his right arm.

Captain Peacock's idea of the perfect holiday is a trip to a nudist colony with a good book.

A Much Sought-After Supporting Actor

Frank Thornton is delighted to say he has absolutely nothing whatsoever in common with Captain Peacock—except that they are the same height. "It is one of the joys of being an actor that you get the chance to play people who are diametrically opposed to yourself," he says. "Like myself, the men who play little dictators such as Peacock are nearly always the ones who wouldn't dream of hurting a fly."

Frank Thornton Ball (his real name) was born in London on January 15, 1921. "As a boy I used to pay 3ð to sit in the front row of the Capitol Cinema in Forest Hill, in South London, to watch Laurel and Hardy. And all the way home by myself, in the dark or the fog, I would be Laurel and Hardy, acting out all their scenes. They were magical days for me," he recalls.

Thornton's interest in music shone through at school. He appeared in productions of *The Mikado* and *Yeomen of the Guard*, and played the cello in the orchestra. After a brief career in insurance, he studied acting at the London School of Dramatic Art and, on April Fool's Day 1940, he made his professional debut in Ireland, taking a tour of four plays around small-town and

3ð

threepence (pronounced "thruppence"), referring to a pre-decimal coin or monetary unit—80 of them in a pound

village halls. It proved an excellent grounding, and the following year, he joined legendary actor/manager Donald Wolfit's Shakespearean company at London's Strand Theater playing, among other parts, Laertes, Bassanio, and Lysander. It was there that Thornton met the woman who was to become his wife, actress Beryl Evans. "She told me that mine was the worst Bassanio she had ever witnessed," he laughs. In spite of that review, they married four years later and are still together. They have a 29-year-old daughter, Jane, who is a stage manager.

During the Second World War, Thornton appeared in John Gielgud's production of *Macbeth* and Terence Rattigan's *Flare Path,* also finding time to make Allied propaganda broadcasts and spend three-and-a-half years in the Royal Air Force.

Thornton's flair for comedy began to surface in the 1950s when he worked in repertory theater, touring shows, and West End productions with such accomplished comedians as Robertson Hare, Ralph Lynn, Alfred Drayton, and Arthur Riscoe. As television started to make its mark in Britain, he appeared with the great Tony Hancock in the comedy classic *Hancock's Half Hour.*

"Because of my height [6 feet 2 inches], I tended to be cast in comedies as aloof, somewhat superior characters, men in authority," he explains. "I suppose that made me quite a good foil."

In 1960, Michael Bentine's revue *Don't Shoot—We're English* gave rise to the television series *It's a Square World.* The latter was one of the finest examples of madcap British humor, a precursor to the likes of *Monty Python's Flying Circus.* Bentine was supported by an able cast, including Thornton, Ronnie Barker, Clive Dunn of *Dad's Army* fame, and Benny Lee, who, 21 years later, would be reunited with Thornton in *Are You Being Served?* in the short-lived role of Mr. Klein.

It's a Square World established Thornton as one of the most sought-after supporting actors for comedy series. He appeared

regularly with Terry Scott and then teamed up with Spike Milligan for the splendid *World of Beachcomber*. The situation suited him well. "I have always liked being a supporting man. If I was given, say, *The Frank Thornton Show,* my great fear would be that the public would become fed up with me," admits Thornton. "Also, fame on television can be overrated. The pleasure of having bus drivers recognize your face doesn't exactly pay the rent. If I'd been part of the American system—where you do something like 39 episodes of a show each year—I'd be rolling in money. But the BBC system does only six or seven a year. It is impossible to make a living on that, so you have to go off and work in the theater.

"*Are You Being Served?* has always appealed to me because I am part of a team," continues the unassuming Thornton. "There is no star as such. We all **muck in** together. Whenever we meet up again, we're always glad to see one another, which makes for a marvelous working atmosphere. Trying to do comedy if you're forever fighting and arguing would be a terrible grind. In *Are You Being Served?*, all the petty jealousies are confined to the characters on-screen—there's none of it among the cast."

After all those years as a supporting man in a variety of roles, Thornton was amazed to find himself suddenly identified with just one character, Captain Peacock. "I'd always been considered a versatile character actor and suddenly I was Captain Peacock. It was a bit strange."

What has also been surprising to Thornton is the success of *Are You Being Served?* in America. "For years everybody said, 'There's no use in trying to sell this show to America, they won't like this sort of thing. They won't understand it.' Now we are absolutely knocked out by the extraordinary reaction to it. We've never pretended that *Are You Being Served?* is a great social document, but I hope it's solid entertainment."

(to) muck in
to help out or pitch in

Beyond Are You Being Served?

"The first I knew about *Grace and Favour* was when Jeremy Lloyd rang me up and said, 'We've got this idea about moving the staff of Grace Brothers to the country. How do you feel about it?' I said, 'Are you and David writing it?' He said, 'Yes.' I said, 'I'll do it.' I always think it's important to keep the same writers on a show. I hate it when series are turned over to a committee. The end product is never as satisfactory—the show invariably seems to become bland."

Thornton's work was a steady stream of comedy, Chekhov, and Shakespeare (he has played Sir Andrew Aguecheek in *Twelfth Night* and Duncan in *Macbeth,* both with the Royal Shakespeare Company, as well as Leonato in *Much Ado About Nothing* in the West End and John of Gaunt in *Richard II* at the prestigious Ludlow Festival in Shropshire). In addition, he found time to return to one of his first loves—opera. In 1982, he appeared in opera for the first time since his schooldays, as the First Lord of the Admiralty in Gilbert and Sullivan's *HMS Pinafore.*

"I had to take singing lessons for that," Thornton admits, "and since then I have done quite a few musicals. Early in 1992, I did a show called *Spread a Little Happiness,* which was a celebration of the songs of Vivian Ellis. It was quite an experience, singing for my living at the age of 71."

Off-screen, Thornton is a quiet, rather serious man and a keen conservationist. He enjoys birdwatching, being with his grandchildren, and occasionally visiting family friends in Montana. But regardless of his great range of interests and acting roles, he will always be known to many as Captain Peacock. As recently as November 1994, Marcus Berkman, television critic for the *Daily Mail,* in reviewing the BBC's blockbuster adaptation of Charles Dickens' novel *Martin Chuzzlewit,* remarked that the cast included Nicholas Smith, Mr. Rumbold from *Are You Being Served?* "But," added the critic sadly, "there was no sign of Captain Peacock."

The Bed Sitting Room
The Magic Christian
The Private Life of Sherlock Holmes
Up the Chastity Belt
No Sex Please—We're British
Digby the Biggest Dog in the World
The Three Musketeers
Are You Being Served?
Old Dracula
The Bawdy Adventures of Tom Jones
The Old Curiosity Shop
(some 60 films in all)

THEATER CREDITS INCLUDE
Twelfth Night
Macbeth
Shut Your Eyes and Think of England
Bedroom Farce
Habeas Corpus
HMS Pinafore
Dial M for Murder
Last of the Red Hot Lovers
Are You Being Served?
Me and My Girl
Richard II
The Pirates of Penzance
The Tutor
Winnie
Peter Pan
Much Ado About Nothing
It Runs in the Family
Don't Shoot—We're English

TREVOR BANNISTER

as

Mr.

Lucas

JUNIOR SALESMAN IN
GENTLEMEN'S READY-TO-WEAR

1972 – 1979

WHEN *ARE YOU BEING SERVED?* BEGAN, MR. LUCAS HAD BEEN the junior in the menswear department for less than two months. His first name varied from James to Dick, although, given his hobbies, the latter was surely more appropriate.

It might come as a surprise to learn that Mr. Lucas passes many a pleasant hour in the local library. Not reading books, though—he likes to loiter with intent between *Fanny Hill* and *Lady Chatterley's Lover* and ask women why they don't try practice instead of theory. He says they daren't slap him because of the signs saying "Silence."

He has no shortage of girlfriends. He tells of one who started groping for the passenger-door handle half a mile from home. So before he asked her out again, he unscrewed the handle. (He calls this technique "Clunk Click Strip Off Quick.") Another girlfriend had thin blood, and Mr. Lucas felt obliged to stay with her overnight to keep her circulation flowing during a cold spell.

Most of his energies are concentrated in a fruitless pursuit of Miss Brahms. He only makes a pass at her in the first place because his regular girlfriend has caught the measles. When he finally lures Miss Brahms to his place, she, too, ends up with measles. He asks Miss Brahms to stay with him while his mother is away, promising her that she can stay in the spare room. He fails to mention that he lives in the spare room.

"Trevor Bannister is a fine actor.
He somehow managed to be dread-
fully rude to Mrs. Slocombe without
being unpleasant. It was wonderful for
me, because it gave Mrs. Slocombe
something to bite back at."
—Mollie Sugden

In the first couple of episodes, Mr. Lucas is complimentary toward Mrs. Slocombe but soon starts making her the butt of his jokes. As a result of this, she turns against him. Captain Peacock is singularly unimpressed by Mr. Lucas' work rate and tries to get him sacked. In the period leading up to the episode "Our Figures Are Slipping," Mr. Lucas has made just three sales. He tries to pick up a few hints from Mr. Humphries for kneeing trousers, but when he attempts the maneuver, he puts his knee right through the seat.

The one thing at which Mr. Lucas does excel is spinning a good yarn—especially when Mr. Rumbold is on the point of giving him a **dressing down** for his appallingly erratic punctuality. On one occasion, he recounts a dream he claims to have had in which he arrived at the store to find everyone motionless. Captain Peacock shattered when he touched him. He says he spent so long trying to put the captain back together again that he overslept. In an equally inventive excuse, he explains that he had arrived at work on time but had seen a military-looking gentleman knocked down in the road. Thinking it was Captain Peacock, he had rushed back to help, thus being delayed. Another tale he uses to gain sympathy is the creation of a household even more bizarre than that of the Addams Family. When in trouble, he reels out the grandfather with the iron lung, the crippled mother, and the asthmatic cat.

A Serendipitous Collision with David Croft

At the start of *Are You Being Served?,* Trevor Bannister was fresh from his success as a dubious character called Heavy Breathing in *The Dustbinmen,* a situation comedy set around a team of **council** garbage collectors and their **cart,** Thunderbird Three. When screened in 1969, the first six episodes of the show all reached No. 1 in the ratings.

dressing down
a reprimand

council
local authorities who organize services—such as garbage collection; in 1970s sitcoms council workers were portrayed as lazy

cart
garbage truck

"That was my first television comedy," recalls Bannister, "and it gave me the taste for more. A couple of years later, I was in a Roy Cooney farce in the West End called *Move Over, Mrs. Markham*, which was nearing the end of its run. During a break, I popped into a London club and happened to bump into David Croft. I had never even met him before, although obviously I knew of his work, but he offered me this script for a pilot show set in a department store. I took it away, read it, and liked it, particularly because the character he wanted me to play, Mr. Lucas, seemed very much the main character. In the early episodes of *Are You Being Served?*, everything revolved around Lucas—he was the one who was always getting into trouble."

When Bannister joined the cast of *Are You Being Served?* he had no idea how long it would last. "None of us knew that it would run and run, but in any case, we all got along so well together that it was a pleasure to go into work each day," he recalls.

National Service
military service

A Versatile, Productive Chap

Trevor Bannister was born in Durington, Wiltshire. There is a history of comedy in his family: His grandfather was "feed," or straight, man to the famous music hall comic Little Titch. Bannister left school at 15, but despite having shown an interest in amateur dramatics, he found his parents objecting to his pursuing a career on the stage. He went into his father's wholesale newspaper business for a year before realizing his dream and being accepted by the London Academy of Music and Dramatic Art.

After that, he put in two years of National Service stationed in Nigeria—and then a number of years in repertory. He made his London stage debut in *The World of Suzie Wong*. Shortly afterward, he took over from Albert Finney in *Billy Liar*. Then *The Dustbinmen* introduced him to a wider audience. Between series of *Are You Being Served?*, he played the villainous Colonel

Masters in the science fiction series *The Tomorrow People,* an indication of Bannister's versatility, which is matched by his productivity. He has made more than 500 appearances in theater, films, and television, ranging from Shakespeare to farce to pantomime. But it is as Mr. Lucas that he is still best known.

"The reaction from *The Dustbinmen* was phenomenal," he says. "It was virtually impossible to go shopping. But, if anything, *Are You Being Served?* was even more popular. It was particularly big in Holland, as a result of which we were often asked to pop over and open shops there. I remember one such trip to Utrecht. There were crowds waiting to greet us at the airport, and we were driven through the streets in a motorcade of open-top vintage cars. There must have been 20,000 people lining the roadside. We felt like pop stars. They kept throwing flowers at us and with the cars being open-topped, we soon found ourselves up to our waists in flowers. I've been out to Australia, too, and always got a good reaction there. I find that whenever I go into a shop, the assistants are dying to say to me, 'Are you being served?'"

Exiting *Are You Being Served?*

In 1979, Bannister made the difficult decision to say farewell to Mr. Lucas. "I have always been a little wary of being in things for too long—there is that constant fear of becoming typecast. But *Are You Being Served?* wasn't too bad," he admits. "It only took seven weeks a year to do and that left me plenty of time to concentrate on theater work. Anyway, I was offered a tour of the West End play *Middle-Age Spread,* and it was something I really wanted to do. Unfortunately, the dates of the tour clashed with the recording dates of *Are You Being Served?*, but the play management very kindly rearranged the tour itinerary so that I would always be near enough to London to get to the BBC to do *Are You Being Served?* on Sunday. But the BBC then changed the recording day

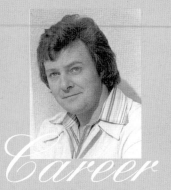

Career
HIGHLIGHTS

TV CREDITS INCLUDE
Country Matters

The War of Darkie Pilbeam

The Dustbinmen

Sullen Sisters

The Tomorrow People

A Voyage Round My Father

Lucky Jim

Call Earnshaw

Hilary

Wyatt's Watchdogs

The Saint

Cider with Rosie

The Upper Hand

Doomsday Gun

Keeping Up Appearances

Woof

FILM CREDITS INCLUDE
Are You Being Served?

from Sunday to Friday, so we clashed all over again. I was left with the choice of the play or the series, and I chose the play."

Bannister admits it wasn't just scheduling conflicts that led to his decision. "To be honest, I felt that *Are You Being Served?* was beginning to repeat itself—the same jokes were cropping up again. I thought there was a danger that it might outstay its welcome. To my mind, *Dad's Army* also went on longer than it should have. Ironically, my favorite episode was one of the last I did. It was 'The Punch and Judy Affair,' where Wendy Richard and I were Punch and Judy. Alfie Bass was in it, too. It was a wonderfully silly episode."

He sees that episode as being an example of the show at its best, "when it was being really silly. It was seaside-postcard, pantomime stuff. It was light, frivolous escapism. There was nothing deep and meaningful about it—for example, nobody ever explained to me why we'd all suddenly burst into a dance routine. It wasn't really a true sitcom like *Till Death Us Do Part* or *Steptoe and Son,* both of which combined comedy with pathos and had characters with depth. The characters in *Are You Being Served?* were pretty superficial. There was no depth to them. All I ever did was chase Miss Brahms. We knew nothing much about our backgrounds."

Having said that, Bannister adds, "I did enjoy playing Lucas. He was a fun character—a 𝔍𝔞𝔠𝔨-𝔱𝔥𝔢-𝔩𝔞𝔡—and I quite liked him, although I think the only thing we had in common was a sense of humor."

Now 59, Bannister lives in Surrey with his second wife, Pamela. Since he left *Are You Being Served?,* he has been constantly in demand, appearing on stage in the United States, Canada, Australia, Holland, the Far East, and the Middle East. He has also toured extensively in Britain. Like John Inman, he is a stalwart of the Christmas pantomime season and has played *Dame* for more

𝔍𝔞𝔠𝔨-𝔱𝔥𝔢-𝔩𝔞𝔡
one who is the most conspicuous in a group, usually a charming troublemaker

than 15 years at various venues throughout the country. He has had his own radio series, *Oh My Sainted Aunt,* and has appeared regularly on television in comedy series such as *Hilary* and *Wyatt's Watchdogs.*

"I certainly don't regret leaving *Are You Being Served?* when I did. The show was absolutely right for the time. It was wonderfully irreverent and covered topics with a wide brush without getting too heavy or involved. People loved the series because it had a huge amount of charm. But times change, and we wouldn't get away with it today, because it was so close to the knuckle. Basically, Lucas was just a sexist with no respect for women at all. A character like that would not be acceptable today. That's why—even if I had been asked—I would not have been interested in doing *Grace and Favour.* For a start, you should never go back to things once you've left, but also I could never resurrect Lucas. He might have been OK as a bottom-pinching 30-year-old, but now, 20 years on, he'd just be seen as a dirty old man."

"I was a terrible giggler—I still am—and so is Wendy Richard. It didn't take much for us to set each other off. Apart from anything else, we never knew what color Mollie's hair would be each week!"—Trevor Bannister

Mr. *Rumbold*

STORE MANAGER CUTHBERT RUMBOLD IS CALLED "JUG EARS" behind his back. As he approaches the menswear department, he looks like a cab with the doors open. For a man in a senior executive position, he feels he has to keep his ear to the ground. He has the advantage of being able to do so without kneeling down.

It is not only his physical appearance that makes him a figure of fun at Grace Brothers. Rumbold believes he is God's gift to management, an inspiration to those beneath him, a leader of men. He is convinced that tact and sensitivity are his strong points, but he is totally lacking in either quality, even though he has attended endless seminars and meetings on management. The truth is he couldn't be counted on to run a bath, let alone a business.

Born in 1924, Rumbold served in the Army Catering Corps during the Second World War. He attained his present lofty rank at Grace Brothers after graduating from the Hardware Department.

A model of vigilance, Rumbold is always on his guard against petty pilfering and accordingly keeps his most valued possessions, his teacup and **biscuits**, in his office safe. He is also an incurable hypochondriac. In the episode "Big Brother" in season two, management decides to install a surveillance system to apprehend shoplifters. Needless to say, the staff are none too keen on being spied upon and seize the opportunity to convince Rumbold that the stress of using the surveillance cameras is shortening his life.

biscuits
cookies, when referred to as "sweet biscuits" or "tea biscuits"; plain biscuit (used, for example, to serve with cheese) often refers to crackers

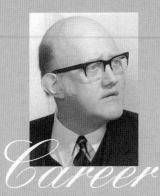

Rumbold would appear to have all the sex appeal of a constipated warthog, yet in "A Personal Problem," from season eight, Captain Peacock becomes convinced that his wife is having an affair with Rumbold, but perhaps it's just wishful thinking on the Captain's part.

A Diverse Career

After seeing Nicholas Smith as the hapless Rumbold, it is hard to believe that when Grace Brothers closes for the day, he can invariably be found performing in musicals. Smith sings a high baritone and is also an accomplished musician, having mastered the piano, trumpet, guitar, and drums. Indeed, he began his show business career in musicals.

After leaving London's Royal Academy of Dramatic Art in 1957, he studied singing with Emelie Hooke, a decision that quickly paid dividends as he earned roles in *The Beggar's Opera*, a tour of *The Desert Song*, and a tour of *Me and My Girl* with Lupino Lane, the British comedian famed for his American two-reeler films in the 1920s. This was one of Lane's last performances before his death in 1959.

Throughout the sixties, Nicholas Smith continued to combine singing and acting. He sang on a British tour of the American musical *Go for Your Gun* and appeared in such diverse productions as *The Avengers, Doctor Who* (in a six-part story called "The Dalek Invasion of Earth"), and commercials for **potato crisps**, ice cream, and coffee.

potato crisps
potato chips

He had shown quite a flair for comedy, playing figures of authority in David Frost's *The Frost Report,* and in 1970, he was cast as Hidius in the Roman romp *Up Pompeii!,* starring Frankie Howard. *Up Pompeii!* had more than its share of innuendo, so it served as a solid grounding when, two years later, Smith was chosen to play Rumbold in the *Comedy Playhouse* pilot of *Are You Being Served?*

"*Up Pompeii!* was rife with double entendres," says Smith, "and of course it's the same with *Are You Being Served?* But it's harmless enough. In my view, provided there's a clean meaning to a line and the actors are seen to believe in that meaning, then it's all right. It's all a matter of how you play it. In *Are You Being Served?*, we played it with great innocence. In fact, when it comes to talking about *Are You Being Served?*, the public generally says to me, 'Mr. Smith, what a lovely clean show it is.'"

Nicholas Smith had another running part in the 1970s—as Police Constable Jeff Yates in *Z Cars*. He has also appeared in Masterpiece Theater's *A Tale of Two Cities*, films such as *Dr. Jekyll and Mr. Hyde, The Adventures of Sherlock Holmes' Smarter Brother,* and *Salt and Pepper,* with Sammy Davis, Jr. In 1983, he played *The Mikado* in the West End production of Gilbert and Sullivan's opera, and the following year performed in his own one-man show, *An Evening with Nicholas Smith.* Now 60, he lives in South London with his wife, Mary.

"*Rumbold is a bit of an oaf, certainly not someone you'd trust to run a large department store with any degree of efficiency, but I've always thoroughly enjoyed playing him.*"—Nicholas Smith

FILM CREDITS INCLUDE
Partners in Crime
Those Magnificent Men in Their Flying Machines
Salt and Pepper
The Canterbury Tales
Are You Being Served?
Dr. Jekyll and Mr. Hyde
Tea and Bullets

THEATER CREDITS INCLUDE
Are You Being Served?
Me and My Girl
Go for Your Gun
Sleeping Beauty
Portrait of a Queen
Marriage Unlimited
Aladdin
Cinderella
As You Like It
Outside Edge
St. Joan
A Midsummer Night's Dream
The Mikado
My Fair Lady
The Plantagenets
The Mousetrap

65

ARTHUR BROUGH

as

Mr.

Grainger

SENIOR SALESMAN IN
GENTLEMEN'S READY-TO-WEAR
1972 – 1977

ERNEST GRAINGER IS THE CRUSTY SENIOR SALESMAN IN GENTLE-men's Ready-to-Wear. He joined Grace Brothers at the age of 28 on the day— May 28, 1937—Stanley Baldwin was replaced as British prime minister by Neville Chamberlain. He spent two years on the ground floor in Haberdashery before moving on to his own counter in Stationery. He then spent five years in Bathroom Furnishings (probably something to do with his bladder) and passed through Gentlemen's Shoes before ending up in Gentlemen's Trousers.

He is fiercely territorial. When he learns that after 25 years of occupying the entire first floor his department is going to have to surrender a large amount of floor space to Ladies' Separates and Underwear, he is suitably indignant. This leads to an ongoing conflict with the equally unyielding Mrs. Slocombe, high-lighted in the episode "His and Hers" from the first season. Mrs. Slocombe isn't going to take this lying down, something she has made a lifetime habit of doing.

Very much set in his ways, Mr. Grainger is appalled to discover in "Hoorah for the Holidays" that management is changing next year's holiday dates. He and Mrs. Grainger have been going to Mrs. Featherstone's boardinghouse in Little-hampton for years, and he fears that a cancellation might lead to his being blacklisted by LALA, the Littlehampton Landladies' Association. Never seen in public without his tape measure, Mr. Grainger is a master of the salesman's philosophy that any garment that may appear too long will ride up with wear.

"[Arthur Brough] was a great deal of fun with a tremendous sense of humor. He was always getting up to mischievous pranks of some sort. Unfortunately, he was very bad with names and could never remember any in the script. Once he had to say Oscar Peterson, and he tried all manner of variations on the name without getting it right!"—Mollie Sugden

"Arthur had spent years and years in rep theaters, and always kept a bag of sweets in his jacket pocket. It used to drive the costume girls round the twist, because when the next show came up to go into studio, they'd find these boiled sweets stuck to the lining of his jacket from the previous week. Nobody ever said anything though, because they loved him so much."—Clive Parker, a former BBC production assistant

"I remember old Mr. Grainger, Arthur Brough, coming up to me and saying 'Am I going to be on for a minute?' and if I said 'No, I don't think you are,' we'd let a few minutes pass and then we'd all stand by the window at North Acton (the rehearsal rooms) and watch as he'd scuttle off to the pub for a quick little refresher. When he came back in, he was always in top form. He was a wonderful character. He was still in very good health and also incredibly funny. Very alive."
—Bob Spiers, director

As a result of his advanced years, Mr. Grainger has a tendency to fall asleep at the most inopportune moments. On one occasion when he dozes off at his post, Mr. Humphries explains that he is really listening for the sound of woodworms in the counter. After doing anything remotely taxing, he has to be revived with a glass of water, invariably ordered by Mr. Lucas.

round the twist
crazy

Fame Comes After Retirement

Fame came late in life to Arthur Brough—in fact, 13 years after he had officially retired. He had been a stalwart of repertory theater for more than 50 years but did not make his television debut until he was given a small part in *Dad's Army*.

"I only had to say a couple of words," he recalled, "but it was enough." David Croft spotted him and plunged him into the limelight as Mr. Grainger in *Are You Being Served?* The irony was not lost on Brough, who remarked, "For so many years I played to audiences of hundreds and then suddenly I am known to millions. It absolutely astounds me."

Brough was born Frederick Arthur Baker, confusingly the son of a butcher. He wanted to be a teacher, but, unable to find a teaching job, he worked in a solicitor's office instead. Office work was too mundane for him, and he began to take a keen interest in the theater. His parents urged him to continue in steady employment, but, on his twenty-first birthday, he overcame their opposition and joined the Royal Academy of Dramatic Art.

In 1929, he married Elizabeth Addyman at Seaford in Sussex, and a few weeks later, with just £50 in their pockets, they launched a repertory company at the Leas Pavilion, Folkestone, Kent. Elizabeth also became his stage partner. Remembering those early days, he said, "We used to look through a small hole in the curtain and assess the value of the house. If it was £20, we were delighted!"

Brough was one of the pioneers of repertory theater in England, and his name became inextricably linked with Folkestone. In his honor, the town named a repertory company after him, the Arthur Brough Players, and several of its members went on to do major TV and film jobs. Brough was much loved by the cast of *Are You Being Served?*, says Trevor Bannister. "He had a wicked sense of humor and we all adored him."

On Easter in 1978, his wife, Elizabeth, died. To lose his stage partner and domestic partner after so many years came as such a blow that Arthur Brough felt he could no longer continue acting. He quit *Are You Being Served?* and within two months of his wife's demise, he died at their home in Folkestone at the age of 73.

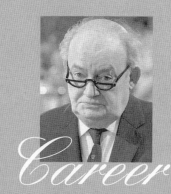

Career

HIGHLIGHTS

FILM CREDITS INCLUDE
Are You Being Served?

THEATER CREDITS INCLUDE
*Numerous parts
in repertory theater
productions over more
than 50 years*

HAROLD BENNETT

as

Young Mr.
Grace

STORE OWNER
19**72** — 19**81**

GRACE
BROS.

YOUNG MR. GRACE IS A PHENOMENON OF THE RETAIL TRADE.

Even though he hasn't been young since the reign of Queen Victoria, he still loves to 𝔥𝔬𝔩𝔦𝔡𝔞𝔶 in St. Tropez, go scuba diving, and pay frequent visits to his favorite club—Fiona's Body Building Massage Parlour. He lives life in the fast lane when really he should be living it in the bus lane. The question is, can he keep it up? But at his age, that would always be a problem. His every need is attended to by a succession of young nurses. His blood pressure rises in unison with their hemlines.

Behind that frail figure lurks a veritable tyrant. He rules Grace Brothers with a rod of iron and is not afraid to make unpopular decisions. It was he who wanted the store to open at 8:30 a.m., a bitter blow to Mrs. Slocombe, who desperately needed her beauty sleep. There was also the introduction of the closed-circuit cameras, the holiday closedown, and, in "Shedding the Load" from season six, the threat of 𝔯𝔢𝔡𝔲𝔫𝔡𝔞𝔫𝔠𝔦𝔢𝔰. When gossip spreads about Captain Peacock and Mr. Rumbold's secretary after the Christmas party, Young Mr. Grace steps in swiftly and convenes a board of inquiry, which promises to be second in severity only to the Spanish Inquisition.

But he has what were for him (but perhaps not for others) moments of kindness. Once on his way to the store in his old Rolls, he spots an assistant salesperson running in the rain trying to catch a bus. He orders the chauffeur to stop, and as the bus disappears in a cloud of spray, he rolls down the window

(tɒ) 𝔥𝔬𝔩𝔦𝔡𝔞𝔶
to go on vacation

𝔯𝔢𝔡𝔲𝔫𝔡𝔞𝔫𝔠𝔦𝔢𝔰, 𝔱𝔬
𝔪𝔞𝔨𝔢 𝔯𝔢𝔡𝔲𝔫𝔡𝔞𝔫𝔱
layoffs, to lay off

and says in a kindly voice, "Never mind, there's sure to be another one soon." He recognizes loyalty, and when Mr. Grainger seems to be heading for enforced retirement, Young Mr. Grace turns up to wish him many more happy years with the firm. He clearly also has a soft spot for Mrs. Slocombe (most people's idea of a soft spot for Mrs. Slocombe would be quicksand). When he hears that her new apartment has been occupied by **squatters**, he finds her a vacant one in the Furniture Department. And, of course, he never misses the chance to tell his staff that they have all done very well.

He eventually dies while scuba diving with Miss Lovelock, happily, one assumes.

From Making Lights to Appearing Under Them

Like Arthur Brough, veteran actor Harold Bennett was a comparative latecomer to television fame. Born in Hastings, Sussex, in 1899, he became an apprentice jeweler before turning his attentions to the theater. The Depression years of the early 1930s were hazardous times for a young actor with a family of three children, and so Bennett decided to leave the stage for the security of a job as a designer/draughtsman with a lighting company.

He continued to keep his hand in at acting, appearing as a film extra and in occasional television series such as the 1959 school comedy series *Whacko!* It was not until he retired from the lighting company at the age of 65 that his career entered a true renaissance.

Not surprisingly since he was now in his seventies, he became much in demand for playing old men. His secret was that although he looked frail and feeble both on- and off-screen, his mind was still razor-sharp. Actor Bill Pertwee, who appeared with Harold

Writer Jeremy Lloyd held Harold Bennett in great esteem and thought he was absolutely superb as Young Mr. Grace. He was particularly amused when Bennett, listening to the character breakdown, asked, "Do you want me to use my old man's voice?" Bennett was 73 at the time.

Bennett in *Dad's Army*, noted in his book on the series, "When it came to playing his part, Harold was dominating and forthright without any sign of hesitancy."

Bennett enjoyed the semiregular role of the irascible Mr. Bluett in *Dad's Army*, which inevitably brought him to the attention of that seasoned talent spotter David Croft. In fact, Croft also saw him in a theater production of *The Rose and the Ring* and sensed then that Bennett was the man to play Young Mr. Grace.

Bennett carried off that role with great charm. "Harold was a super person," says Mollie Sugden. "He had a rather naive, innocent quality for all his messing about with the girls. He did it with a sort of childlike quality that somehow wasn't offensive."

During breaks from *Are You Being Served?*, Bennett worked on the television adaptation of Arnold Bennett's *Clayhanger*, an Open University production of Chekhov's *The Three Sisters*, and Franco Zeffirelli's television epic *Jesus of Nazareth*.

By 1981, at age 82, with some 200 television and stage credits to his name, he found that age was finally beginning to catch up with him. He had already recorded the Christmas edition of *Are You Being Served?* but announced that he was taking a rest from the series, adding that he hoped to be back soon. Harold Bennett never returned. On September 15, 1981, he died at his London home.

Career
HIGHLIGHTS

TV CREDITS INCLUDE
Whacko!

Dad's Army

Clayhanger

Jesus of Nazareth

The Three Sisters

FILM CREDITS INCLUDE
Are You Being Served?

THEATER CREDITS INCLUDE
The Rose and the Ring

Mr.

Harman

MAINTENANCE MAN / PORTER

19**76** — 19**85**

BEVERLEY HARMAN SUCCEEDED MR. MASH AS GRACE BROTHERS' maintenance man in 1976. Like his predecessor, he is a stickler for union rules and will happily quote them when it suits him. When Captain Peacock asks him to make a contribution to Mrs. Slocombe's birthday present, he suddenly remembers that he is not allowed on the floor during working hours.

Despite his menial position with the firm, he is not afraid to voice his opinions—even when they're not wanted, which is most of the time. In the episode "Oh What a Tangled Web," it is he who conducts the inquiry into Captain Peacock's alleged infidelity with Miss Hazelwood, displaying a zeal that would have done credit to Perry Mason.

From Spiv to Follyfoot and Beyond

Arthur English's entrée into the acting world came about abruptly. At 10:15 one morning in 1949, English, then 30 years old and a former sergeant instructor in the Royal Army Corps, took time off from his job as a £6-a-week painter and decorator to attend an audition at London's famous Windmill Theatre. Within five minutes, he was told, "You're hired."

Over the next few years, Arthur English perfected the character of the Spiv, the widest of 𝔴𝔦𝔡𝔢 𝔟𝔬𝔶𝔰 who operated in the black market conditions that prevailed during rationing in post-war Britain. On stage, he developed a cocky

𝔴𝔦𝔡𝔢 𝔟𝔬𝔶
one who lives by his wits; a questionable or shady character

Arthur English keeps an autograph book with the signatures of famous variety stars of the 1930s, including those of British comedians Max Miller and Arthur Askey, and he admits, "I'm still stagestruck now."

strut and a machine-gun delivery of 300 words-a-minute. When rationing ended and the black market disappeared, so did the Spiv, and English was forced to find a new act.

But that didn't happen for many years. English drifted along in summer seasons, a seeming relic from the glorious days of music hall. The turning point came in 1971 when he was cast as Slugger, an ex-boxer in the popular children's television series *Follyfoot*. Arthur English had finally found a new career; like many comedians before and since, he had become a straight actor.

"*Follyfoot* was what really started me up again and after that, the parts started to roll in," says English. "I was in *Doctor in the House, Dixon of Dock Green,* and, in 1974, I did a play about an ex-comedian that was specially written for me, called *Clap Hands for the Walking Dead.* It's funny—people always say to me what a big transition it is from comedy to acting, but really I've always considered myself to be a character actor. The Spiv was a character."

Just when things seemed to be going well, English's wife of 34 years passed away, leaving him devastated. But two years later in 1976, he bounced back—not only performing as Mr. Harman in *Are You Being Served?* but also marrying again, to dancer Teresa Mann, who was 35 years his junior.

"I was very low when I met Teresa. My wife had died a couple of years before, and I felt as if I had nothing left," English recalls. "I was pretty sort of stupid. I was drinking a bit heavily—a couple of bottles of whisky a day. By then, I had just started in *Are You Being Served?* John Inman and I were chatting one day and he said to me, 'Why don't you come into pantomime with me this year? It's away from people and away from celebrating Christmas.'"

So English took the part of the Squire in *Mother Goose* at Wimbledon in South London. There he met Teresa on the very first night when she and another dancer borrowed his dressing room.

They married the following year. He had no qualms about the age difference, reasoning, "When my father married my mother, he was 35 years older than she. And I was born when he was 65." Soon English had a baby daughter, Clare Louise, to go with Anthony and Ann, his grown-up son and daughter from his first marriage.

His career continued to prosper. "I loved being in *Are You Being Served?* It's always difficult when a new actor joins an established series—you're so worried about **mucking** everything **up**. But the cast were wonderful to me and made me feel at home **straight away**."

He went on to win rave notices as Mr. Doolittle opposite Twiggy's Eliza in a television production of George Bernard Shaw's *Pygmalion* and played an old man with a terminally ill wife in a 1983 television play called *Wayne and Albert*.

Then in 1986, his marriage with Teresa fell apart amidst allegations that he was once again drinking heavily. Sadly, Arthur English's health has deteriorated badly, and he now suffers from emphysema.

(to) muck up
to make a mess
of things

straight away
immediately,
instantly

MIKE BERRY

as

Mr. Spooner

BERT SPOONER JOINED THE MENSWEAR DEPARTMENT AS A junior in 1981, succeeding Mr. Lucas. Unlike the quick-witted Mr. Lucas, he appears to be hard-of-thinking, giving the impression that he is definitely **a few buttons short of a waistcoat.** No wonder Mrs. Slocombe calls him daft.

At one stage, Mrs. Slocombe, Captain Peacock, and Mr. Rumbold are all for sacking him, but he somehow survives to show unexpected prowess as a singer. At the store party, he performs "Chanson d'Amour" with Mr. Rumbold on the accordion, Captain Peacock on piano, and Miss Brahms and Mrs. Slocombe as **backing singers** dressed in outrageous "Babe" costumes. Mr. Spooner's fame spreads so far that he finally senses a new career opening up as a pop star.

Pop Star in Real Life

The year was 1963. Mike Berry and the Outlaws was one of the hottest pop music acts in Britain. They had already had a big hit with "Tribute to Buddy Holly" in 1961 and were now plugging their latest record, *Don't You Think It's Time?* on television's *Thank Your Lucky Stars*.

Mike Berry was 20 at the time. He and his group had topped the bill at the famous Cavern Club in Liverpool with the Beatles as one of the support bands. When the Beatles appeared with Berry's band on *Thank Your Lucky*

a few buttons short of a waistcoat
dull, unintelligent; same as American expression "a few cards short of a full deck"

backing singers
back-up singers

Stars, they were only just making their mark. So when Lennon and McCartney offered to write Berry a song, he was unimpressed and turned down the offer. It's a decision he lived to regret.

"At the time I thought I was the 𝖇𝖊𝖊'𝖘 𝖐𝖓𝖊𝖊𝖘 and the Beatles were unknown," explains Berry. "As songwriters, John and Paul only had 'Love Me Do' to their name, and that was only a very minor hit. So when John offered to write a song for me as we sat around chatting in the dressing room, I really didn't take too much notice."

Mike Berry and the Outlaws went into decline. Berry opted out of the music business and, in 1969, in a moment of madness, invested what capital he had in a partnership to build 𝖗𝖆𝖈𝖎𝖓𝖌 𝖘𝖆𝖑𝖔𝖔𝖓 𝖈𝖆𝖗𝖘. After two years of eating car grease, with no big sponsors in sight to make him rich, he decided it was time to get back to showbiz. He subsequently had top-ten hits in Europe with "Don't Be Cruel" and a re-recording of "Tribute to Buddy Holly." At around the same time, he took on an agent for photographic modeling and acting, and this led to appearances in a wide range of television commercials for everything from razor blades to chocolate bars, perfume to pizzas. While filming one of the commercials, he met director James Hill, who was casting for a new children's television series, *Worzel Gummidge,* about the adventures of a scarecrow. Berry landed the part of the odd-job man, Mr. Peters, resplendent in false mustache, cloth cap, and horn-rimmed glasses. It was a far cry from the Cavern.

In 1980, Berry had his biggest hit ever, selling more than 300,000 copies of "The Sunshine of Your Smile" to earn a silver disc. This was followed by two more hits.

The following year, Berry joined the cast of *Are You Being Served?* as Mr. Spooner and remained for the show's last three seasons. "It was terrific exposure for me," he says, "because it brought me to a much wider audience as an actor. There was a great spirit of

𝖇𝖊𝖊'𝖘 𝖐𝖓𝖊𝖊𝖘
the hottest thing going

𝖗𝖆𝖈𝖎𝖓𝖌 𝖘𝖆𝖑𝖔𝖔𝖓 𝖈𝖆𝖗𝖘
sports cars of some 30 to 40 years ago when sports cars were souped-up saloon (or sedan) cars and little different from racing cars

HIGHLIGHTS

UK DISCOGRAPHY
"Tribute to Buddy Holly"
"Don't You Think It's Time"
"My Little Baby"
"The Sunshine of Your Smile"
"If I Could Only Make You Care"
"Memories"

TV CREDITS INCLUDE
Thank Your Lucky Stars
Worzel Gummidge

THEATER CREDITS INCLUDE
Heaven's Up
Great Balls of Fire

fellowship among the cast—we'd always help each other out. It reminded me a bit of my days with the band. And the writers put my musical background to good use in the very last episode, 'The Pop Star,' where Mr. Spooner discovers a previously hidden talent—singing. That was great fun to do."

In 1990, Berry starred as Captain Beaky in Jeremy Lloyd's musical *Heaven's Up* in London's West End and went on to record a version of Buddy Holly's "Fool's Paradise" for inclusion in the film *Buddy's Song*, which starred Roger Daltrey of The Who. He recently played Archie in the stage show *Great Balls of Fire*. Married and with two children, Berry says his hobbies are playing golf—badly—and fiddling around in his 16-track recording studio at the bottom of his garden.

Mr. Goldberg

HARRY GOLDBERG SERVED AT GRACE BROTHERS FOR THE seventh season only. He had been running a small tailoring business of his own but saw the post of junior in the menswear department at Grace Brothers as a **leg up**. During his job interview, it emerges that he was in the army with Captain Peacock. This causes the gallant captain great consternation since Mr. Goldberg's version of events differs markedly from his own heroic tales. Captain Peacock spent more time shelling peas than shelling the Germans.

With an eye for the **main chance**, Mr. Goldberg blackmails Captain Peacock into giving him the senior assistant's job instead. Thus the Captain has to tread carefully with his new member of staff. He can't afford to upset Mr. Goldberg in case he spills the beans—something else that Peacock was prone to do while serving with the catering corps.

Mr. Goldberg has three major concerns in his life—money, money, and money. If he could make money as well as he makes clothes, he'd be a happy man. In the story "The Agent," he attempts to supplement his income by starting up an employment agency, finding suitable positions for his talented staff. Mr. Humphries, for one, is prepared to bend over backwards to find a good position.

leg up
a boost, a means
of assistance

main chance
a big break

"Mr. Goldberg was a crafty old devil, but you couldn't help but like him."—Alfie Bass

Alfie Bass was a fervent anti-nuclear protester. He once told a policeman that he was a relative of the then-British Prime Minister Harold Macmillan, so he could be allowed through the police cordon at a Ban the Bomb demonstration. The policeman recognized him immediately, laughed, and let him through.

Taking Comedy Very Seriously

Alfie Bass was born in London in 1921, the youngest of ten children, to immigrant Russian parents who had fled their native country to escape the persecution being meted out to Jews. On leaving school, Bass worked for a while in his father's trade of cabinetmaking and put that experience to good use when he joined the Unity Theatre, making sets and scenery. He made his professional acting debut there in 1939 as Izzie in *Plant in the Sun* with Paul Robeson.

In 1947, he appeared in a Shakespeare season at Stratford, performing in *The Merchant of Venice, Hamlet,* and *The Taming of the Shrew.* Four years later, he played Shortie Fisher in the classic British crime comedy *The Lavender Hill Mob,* which starred Alec Guinness.

By this time, Bass was beginning to specialize in comedy roles, usually as a lovable, little rogue. One such example, and the one that brought him fame, was as Private "Excuse Boots" Bisley in the long-running television sitcom *The Army Game.* His catchphrase "Never mind, eh?" caught on with the public and led to a spin-off series, *Bootsie and Snudge.*

In 1968, Bass took over the role of milkman Tevye from Topol in the hit musical *Fiddler on the Roof.* He continued to pop up in television comedies, joining the *Till Death Us Do Part* team when the sagas of Alf Garnett (the English role model for Archie Bunker) were revived and appearing as Mr. Goldberg in the 1979 season of *Are You Being Served?*

Bass took comedy very seriously, expressing the view that "laughter should arise from natural situations, because the roots of comedy are in reality. The foibles of man can be both tragic and comic—and good comedy should also have an element of sadness about it."

It was a sad day for British show business when Bass died on July 15, 1987.

Career
HIGHLIGHTS

FILM CREDITS INCLUDE
The Lavender Hill Mob

Help!
(the Beatles film)

Alfie

Up the Junction

The Revenge of the Pink Panther

Death on the Nile

and 25 more

TV CREDITS INCLUDE
The Adventures of Robin Hood

The Army Game

Bootsie and Snudge

The Goodies and the Beanstalk

Till Death Us Do Part

THEATER CREDITS INCLUDE
The Merchant of Venice

Hamlet

The Taming of the Shrew

Fiddler on the Roof

as

Mr. Mash

MILITANT MAINTENANCE MAN MR. MASH WORKS AT GRACE Brothers for the first three seasons, being replaced by Mr. Harman for the fourth. Mr. Mash's rough-and-ready manner does not exactly endear him to the likes of Mrs. Slocombe. The more familiar he tries to become, the more "posh" Mrs. Slocombe becomes to retain her dignity. Captain Peacock looks down on him, too, and does not think Mr. Mash should be earning sufficient money to go on holiday to the "Seashells," as he calls the Seychelles Islands.

A familiar face in countless British television series, often playing cab drivers or workmen, Cockney actor Larry Martyn was another actor cast in *Are You Being Served?* on the strength of a minor role in *Dad's Army*. Martyn, whose more recent television appearances include the police series *The Bill* and the sitcom *Never the Twain,* died in 1994.

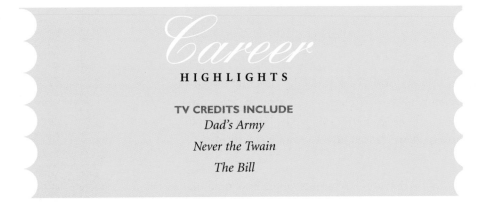

Career

HIGHLIGHTS

TV CREDITS INCLUDE
Dad's Army

Never the Twain

The Bill

as

Old Mr. Grace

GRACE
BROS.

OLD MR. GRACE STEPPED INTO HIS YOUNGER BROTHER'S shoes for season eight when actor Harold Bennett's health began to fail him. Like his brother, Old Mr. Grace has an eye for the girls, who always worried that they might give him a stroke. But that is what he is hoping for.

He has a particular liking for showgirls, and in the episode "Heir Apparent," he spots an old photograph of Mr. Humphries' mother, taken when she was a chorus girl. Recognizing those thighs, he comes to the conclusion that he and Mr. Humphries must be closely, if illegitimately, related. But this is not too surprising: There seems every possibility that Old Mr. Grace has fathered half the population of Western Europe. Very few of his ideas come from above his waist, an exception being his decision to create an in-house magazine. Even then his mind is mainly on the centerfold.

Eternal Old Age

Kenneth Waller is getting used to people telling him to act his age: In series such as *Are You Being Served?* and the ratings-topping sitcom *Bread,* in which he played Grandad, he played characters considerably older than himself.

At 53, Kenneth Waller, who played Old Mr. Grace, was nearly 30 years younger than Harold Bennett, who played Young Mr. Grace.

Kenneth Waller had to mind his language when appearing as Old Mr. Grace for fear of repercussions from his mother, his sternest critic. When he swore on television in his part as Grandad in Bread, his mother was so disgusted that she refused to talk to him for a week.

Career
HIGHLIGHTS

TV CREDITS INCLUDE
South Riding

When We Are Married

The Workhouse Boy

Doctor Who

Coronation Street

Never the Twain,

Juliet Bravo

Big Deal

The Winslow Boy

Bread

FILM CREDITS INCLUDE
Carry On Behind

Room at the Top

Chitty Chitty Bang Bang

Scrooge

Fiddler on the Roof

The Divine Sarah

The Love Pill

THEATER CREDITS INCLUDE
Free As Air

Salad Days

The Solid Gold Cadillac

On the Level

Anne of Green Gables

1776

The Importance of Being Earnest

Entertaining Mr. Sloane

Waller, who is now 67, believes the secret of his eternal old-age lies with his battered nose. "I broke it when I was five years old," he chuckles. "I fell off my little bicycle. But I didn't realize my nose was broken until I was 15 when the hospital took the bone away. My mother screamed, 'Is it going to spoil his good looks?' The doctor replied, 'It won't do him any harm. He's not a girl, is he?' Since then, I've had to build the nose up with putty and plasticine when I'm playing certain parts."

Some 40 years ago, Kenneth Waller **threw up** his day job as an auctioneer's assistant to become an actor in repertory. He gained invaluable experience in the theater but did not really make the breakthrough into television until the 1980s with *Are You Being Served?*, *Big Deal* (in which he played a low-life character called Ferret), and *Bread*.

His role as Grandad in *Bread* earned him a sizable following and also brought him great satisfaction. "It meant I had to turn down a role with the Royal Shakespeare Company at Stratford," he explains. "My agent told them I was too busy doing a new series of *Bread* to go into Shakespeare. It gave me a little twinge of satisfaction to turn them down, because 30 years earlier, I went for an audition with the RSC, and they didn't **want to know** me!"

throw up
give up, quit

want to know
have a use or need for

Simpson
PICCADILLY

New Ideas on Every Level
Mon-Fri 10am-7pm Sat 9.30am-6pm

In the heart of the West End of London, a few hundred yards from Piccadilly Circus, stands Simpson's, one of the most renowned department stores in England. It also happens to be the inspiration for Grace Brothers' department store, equally renowned but for very different reasons. It was at Simpson's that *Are You Being Served?* writer Jeremy Lloyd worked for a time as one of the staff. Any resemblance between the fictional store and its actual counterpart is, therefore, not at all coincidental.

The resemblances are, in fact, many and startlingly uncanny. The **lifts** at Simpson's are centered against the back wall in the middle of the store, just as they are on the set for the television series, and, indeed, many shop assistants stand around waiting for a customer to catch their eye so they can offer help. The architecture is highly stylized and dates from the mid 1930s, when the building was constructed. It's worn so well and is of such significance that it appears on a list of buildings that must be preserved in their original state by mandate. No repair work can be carried out without supervision from restorers, and modernization is simply out of the question.

A constant flow of customers—many of whom are regulars—passes frequently through the many departments. As General Manager John Baylis explains, "We offer a distinct style of service that the customers become used to, and they come back time and time again. One-to-one customer/serviceman relationships develop because we have people working here with definite personalities and character, and they get to know the customers, their tastes, and their styles, making it more relaxing and easier to shop here for them." Shop assistants with "definite personalities and character"? This, too, sounds very familiar.

lift
elevator

Although there was no Young Mr. Grace as such, there certainly was a Mr. Simpson—a Doctor Simpson, in fact—who founded the store more than 60 years ago and brought the business to life.

Even floorwalkers such as Captain Peacock did exist, as Baylis recalls. "The floorwalkers quite literally kept an eye on everything, ensuring that the general operation of running the store was going smoothly. They were the figure of authority on any particular floor for the shop assistants to look to for help or advice," he recalls. "In many cases, there were certainly people working in that position who had a military background. After the Second World War, it was not uncommon for an ex-captain or similar ranking officer to seek out employment in such a way. As with Captain Peacock, they were very strict and authoritative."

Needless to say, Jeremy Lloyd represented another type of employee from a different career background. "I think Jeremy Lloyd took on his position here between jobs, or when he was 'resting,' as the acting profession likes to say," surmises Baylis. "It was not uncommon to find actors in such a position in a department store. Christopher Lee worked at Simpson's for a brief period while he was resting between jobs, and I seem to recall that he was a floorwalker." (But not, presumably, the model for Captain Peacock.)

As for Mr. Humphries' catchphrase, "I'm free!" Baylis feels it could have come from Jeremy Lloyd's time at Simpson's. "He was certainly present during the heyday of the department store trade, when clothing was kept in shelving units, and if the customer wanted to see a particular style of tie, the whole tray was presented for him to choose from. Part of the pleasure of shopping in such a way," he explains, "was that the customer knew that the assistant would offer a discreet opinion of taste, if they so wished, suggesting which pattern of shirt matched a particular style of

(to) queue up
to stand in line
(to wait for
something)

"There were still stores like Grace Brothers in the Are You Being Served? days. Nowadays I think the floorwalker setup may still go on in a few stores. But it's nice to see it. When you don't, it's like missing the corner shop as you queue up at some impersonal checkout."—Jeremy Lloyd

"I knew the show was a real success during the second series, when I went into Austin Reed's (or perhaps it was Harrods) to buy a scarf, and the assistant said to me, 'Can I help you?' I realized then that they'd dropped the phrase, 'Are you being served?' and that my time as a sales assistant had not been wasted."
—Jeremy Lloyd

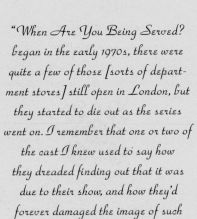

tie. We take pride in the kind of service we offer people who come to shop here, and that was certainly reflected in the program."

The characters of Mr. Grainger and of all the subsequent elderly staff members who appeared in *Are You Being Served?* are not that far from the truth either. Baylis has been with the company since 1968 and admits that some of his staff have also been there for a considerable period.

"We have one gentleman who's been working for us for 46 years, if that gives you some idea," notes Baylis. "Being part of the staff here is very much like being part of an extended family. Employees are here for such a long time that everyone gets to know each other extremely well, and we pride ourselves on the quality of relationships we have with our staff."

Baylis explains how the retail industry, and certainly those working in the department store trade, watched *Are You Being Served?* with a high degree of interest.

"It was followed quite keenly, to be honest, because it directly reflected the industry as a whole, and one was always keen to see how we were being portrayed," he recalls. "In that sense, they got it quite accurate, with the way that they showed the flamboyant characters who certainly work as shop assistants. But [on the show] I think it was a highly concentrated batch—you'd never get that alarming variety of personalities together on one shop floor at any one time. It just doesn't work out that way."

Today at Simpson's, the scene at the lift is most familiar. The lift doors open and a shop assistant steps out with several customers, saying "Ground floor, gentlemen's shirts and ties, ladies' skirts and shoes." A little bit of Grace Brothers still lives on in the heart of London's West End.

CHAPTER

GRACE
BROS.

2

Behind
THE SCENES

SETTING THE
Stage

IN ITS PRIME, THE BBC'S TELEVISION CENTRE WAS a hive of activity with dozens of series and serials being recorded within its eight studios every week.

"It was like a vast **rota**, day in, day out," says Bill McCabe, a former scenic operator at TV Centre. "There was a regular pattern that didn't seem to change for close to 20 years. One day you'd be on a cop show, the next was one of the big chat shows, then day three would be one of the situation comedies. But you never seemed to get the same one twice. There were always about three or four sitcoms recorded every week, and *Are You Being Served?* was part of that system."

The studios at TV Centre are quite literally large empty spaces, soundproofed and lined with hundreds of lights across the ceiling. They vary in size, with TC1 being one of the biggest of its kind in Europe.

The sitcoms are recorded in the larger studios, because those rooms most easily accommodate live audiences. "The studio space was cut in half, literally 50/50," explains McCabe. "The easiest way to explain it is to say that the half nearest the fire exits was where the grandstand (the audience seating) was rigged up, while the half near the scenery doors was where the set went, to allow easy access for any special props or backdrops that were needed for a show."

The drawback, of course, was that the set designer had little space with which to work wonders. "That's partially why there was only ever one main set on most sitcoms, because it's all that there was room for," says McCabe. "*Are You Being Served?* was quite a simple show to set up, because you only ever really

rota
people acting in turn, one after another

The Light Entertainment
DEPARTMENT

The BBC had various departments to handle each type of show, and Are You Being Served? fell under the category of light entertainment, rather than drama series or the more prestigious drama plays. Broadly speaking, anything made by the light entertainment department had to have a family appeal.

Explains Clive Parker, a former BBC production assistant, "Sitcoms were a strange beast, moving from one end of the spectrum, with something like Till Death Us Do Part, which was always broadcast quite late, due to the somewhat politically incorrect nature of the scripts, right to the other extreme, and Are You Being Served? certainly fell under that category. There were plenty of risky innuendoes throughout every episode, but there was an important difference between those two shows.

had the shop floor to rig up. OK, there were the occasional episodes where the canteen or an extra office was needed, but those were just tucked round the back, so those were no real problems.

"There were several exits off the set, which was one unusual aspect we had to cope with. Normally, with something like *Steptoe and Son*, you had a set which was the everyday layout of a house, so the normal rules applied. But there was the odd 'special requirement' for *Are You Being Served?* If John Inman had a quick change, there had to be a quick route to get to the dressing room, so that the audience wasn't kept waiting for too long. It was like those movies where you see someone try to shoot the president, and all the CIA men swarm round him and drag him off like greased lightning. You'd see John get off the side of the set, and the production assistants and costume girls would descend on him like vultures. In a matter of seconds he was back, out of his suit and wearing a sailor's uniform, or something like that."

There were exits through the curtains that led to the "changing rooms" for both the Ladies' and the Men's areas. Six or seven feet back from there was another pair of exits on either side of the set. These supposedly led to offices. And, of course, there was the lift at the back of the set. "This was never a working prop," says McCabe, "because there was no need for one. You never saw the lift rise into view, so it was just a case of having a short flight of stairs backstage for the actors to get into it, and then shutting them in and opening the doors on cue."

There was a cardinal rule that the actors not go beyond the boundaries of the set. "One or two of the directors like to call it the 'Fictional Reality Rule,'" explains McCabe. "They never wanted the actors to step beyond their environment and break the illusion that the audience was watching a real sequence of events unfold in a real setting. Some directors honestly felt frustrated by the fact that there was an audience there, and tried to treat a sitcom like a straight drama."

The set was sometimes a bit intimidating for some of the actors of, shall we say, a certain age. "There was a time we lost Arthur Brough [Mr. Grainger], because he'd tried to find his entrance, and with the lights off round the back of the scenery, he'd gone through the main doors at the back and gotten lost in the scenery corridor," recounts Clive Parker, a former BBC production assistant. "He missed his cue to walk on set, and John [Inman] had to ad-lib for a few minutes while we went and found him. Afterward, he wandered past muttering to himself, saying 'If the white rabbit [from *Alice in Wonderland*] was an actor, he'd have got lost here as well.'"

THE SHOP SHOW IS A SUPER SELL-OUT!

IT'S TELEVISION'S slowest success story. Are You Being Served?, the comedy series about life in a department store, ran for two years without causing much of a stir.

But now it has captured a regular place in telly's Top 20—and with a repeat series, at that.

Actor John Inman, 35, took a walk down Regent Street, in London, a few days ago, and I was mobbed.

"I have to travel everywhere by taxi now. I've been in acting for 25 years, but nothing like this happened to me before."

Are You Being Served? first entered the Top 20 a month ago in 12th place.

A couple of weeks ago, it shot up to third, behind This Is Your Life and the No 1 programme, Love Thy Neighbour.

By PHILIP PHILLIPS

Sweet

This is the highest a BBC comedy series has reached since Porridge, starring Ronnie Barker got the second spot last October.

In recent years, only Steptoe And Son, Porridge, Till Death Us Do Part, and Some Mothers Do 'Ave 'Em, have achieved this sort of success for a BBC comedy.

It was a sweet taste of success for Inman, 50-year-old Mollie Sugden—she plays dragonlike Mrs Slocombe, of ladies' wear—and the rest of the cast.

Why has Are You Being Served? suddenly hit the jackpot?

Writers J... Lloyd... with 44...

who plays the effeminate Mr Humphries, says: "I... true. I've met 'em all in my time."

One showbusiness personality with fond memories of his days as a shop assistant is female impersonator Bunny Lewis.

He says: "The Manchester store I worked in was full of characters.

"But nothing was as funny as the day I got fired when I was demonstrating a pressure cooker. It blew up and covered a large display...

Mr Humphries, says: "I... with rice pudding."

And what does Mary Whitehouse think of the series?

She said yesterday: "I think it's a light-hearted comedy which is funny, often fresh in ideas—and few could take offence at it. I certainly don't."

★ HAVE you ever set foot in a store like the one in Are You Being Served? Tell us what happened to you. Write to Served, The Sun, 30 Bouverie Street, London, EC4Y 8DF. £1 for replies published.

The Sun, May 3, 1975

After a decade as a comedy performer and writer, Jeremy Lloyd saw in Are You Being Served? the opportunity to fill half an hour per week of television with his previous experiences as a junior in a London department store. But the show became much more than that—an extraordinarily popular series that confirmed Lloyd as one of Britain's best-known sitcom writers. The first in a series of successes, Are You Being Served? established Lloyd's partnership with David Croft and inaugurated a writing method that served them well throughout this series and carried them through several more.

How would you go about writing episodes for Are You Being Served?

We'd begin on a Monday and we'd finish by Friday, sometimes by Thursday. We'd write one a week, so we'd have time to think of an idea over the weekend. Then we'd sit down at ten o'clock on Monday with a coffee and ask ourselves what we were going to do that week. Nothing too structured, because whereas in America they like to structure [a show] with every facet of the story defined in the story line, we'd find that very constraining. We were more likely to say, "Let's do a show where it's foggy, and they can't go home. And because they can't go home, they'll have to borrow some tents from the camping department, and an **electric fire**." And that's the basis of the whole show.

You'd outline no more than that, because the dialogue is the fun—some of them would be for [camping out], some would be against it, there'd be problems because they'd have to borrow clothes from the display, which have only got one leg to ensure people won't steal them. We'd get all the fun out of the slimmest of story lines.

electric fire
an electric heater

[Because] the shows were very loosely structured, one had complete freedom within that structure to go off into a conversation about something else altogether. It might be a letter Mrs. Slocombe got from a friend, which has nothing to do with the show at all, but which she'll read. We might start out with one idea and then change it completely, so we'd end up with a different show than the one we were expecting. We were flying by the seat of our writing pads, really.

The "we" being you and David Croft?

Yes. We used to take it in turns to write. For a while, he'd have the pad and I'd do the jokes. Then we'd swap over. Toward the end, I tended to spend less time with the pad than David, because my writing was slower than his. We had great fun, which I think comes across. It was as much fun writing it as it would have been seeing it after someone else had written it. We laughed as much as the audience laughed as the jokes arrived in our minds. His wife always knew whether the show was going well by the amount of laughter [coming] from the study. Sometimes there'd be a tremendous burst of laughter and then David would say, "But we can't say that."

How did you and David Croft get together?

David and I really met on a show I did with Joanna Lumley, *It's Awfully Bad for Your Eyes, Darling,* where we did some cowriting when he was called in to produce. When I had the idea for *Are You Being Served?,* I just sent it to him, outlining my life at Simpson's and suggesting we might collaborate. He liked the idea, because it fell into the area that he liked working with—hierarchical conflict.

How would you go about setting off that conflict?

The characters are perfect for conflict because they have their set positions in life, and so if anyone oversteps the boundaries, that would set it off. If Mrs. Slocombe decides that it's so cold that she's going to wear a pair of men's long johns, Captain Peacock says she's not allowed, even though she can only be seen from the waist up [when she's] behind the counter. "I'm afraid the rules will not permit it. You must be dressed correctly," he would say. So she says she will have to go over his head.

The early episodes have something of a documentary feel in places.

Well, these are things that actually happened while I worked in a department store, which Simpson's would deny, but which did happen. Kneeing a jacket was a technique known by the assistants but not by management. It was sort of autobiographical—sleeves will ride up with wear, breathing on the tape, etc. I had three years' experience at Simpson's, so I poured as much of my own experiences into the show so as to make it authentic. Once we ran out of my experiences, the characters had become so firmly established that one didn't need to go back to learn more about a store. Having created the store and the characters, the stories then became more personal.

Did you ever run out of stories?

We never seemed to be short of stories, and if we were, we would write a thing like "German Week," where the whole point was to try and get the characters into lederhosen so they could do the slap and tickle dance. We can put Mr. Humphries into shorts, and Captain Peacock into lederhosen, which he's told will give him an air of authority, but he finds they give him a lot of air and very little authority.

How closely did the BBC supervise and censor you?

We had nobody overseeing us when the shows were made—there was nobody above David Croft and myself to keep an eye on the scripts. So we were our own censors: It was entirely up to us how far we could go with jokes or humor. Had we done anything unacceptable, we would have been responsible. The BBC never read the scripts; they only saw the show if they happened to drop in to see it being recorded. As we always had an overflowing audience for it, they just knew that they had a successful show and allowed us carte blanche to do what we liked. They relied on our taste not to upset anybody, and as far as I know, we never did—except that we upset a midget once. I'm amazed to hear some episodes have had trouble in America.

A few episodes generated criticism because of a certain insensitivity—at least by some American standards—to racial issues. But generally, the show has had overwhelming success in the States. It's the most popular program on many PBS stations. Were you surprised by this success, with an audience used to more highbrow programs?

Well, it is highbrow, because it's almost historical. It appeals in the same way as *Upstairs Downstairs.* It's set in a time warp where people have a pecking order of politeness and charm, which almost goes back to the 1930s but has disappeared now. People like to see those social strata in which everybody knew their place and were quite happy. Although they fought against it occasionally, the whole structure worked.

The humor is often indirect as well, forcing the audience to use their intelligence.

Yes, it's not jokes per se, but when Mrs. Slocombe tries the youth cream, no one wants to tell her that it's worn off, so they ask her if she's seen *Lost Horizon.* "You remember that when that person got halfway down the tunnel, they got older. Well, you're halfway down the tunnel." It's not being directly rude to anybody.

Was it difficult to retain the credibility of the series as it went on? In "The Hold-Up," for example, it's difficult to believe that the burglars would believe Mr. Humphries was an infamous gangster.

Yes, I think you're right, but I wrote that without my partner, and we're better together than alone. [That episode] provided an excuse to dress Mr. Humphries up, and that got a lot of laughs. It gave him an opportunity to play a character. But I agree with you that once you [get to the point of] Mr. Humphries playing a gangster, it's hardly believable, and then it becomes mere sketch comedy. I decided to do it, I did it, and it got laughs. But it stopped soon after, because one felt that if one had to look for wilder plots, the integrity of what had gone before would be spoiled.

Did the characters develop in unexpected ways?

You never know when you start quite what you're going to do with them. You know you've got the right character, but not what they're going to do or how much they're going to do in a season. Sometimes it's much better to have a strong character that pops in and out of a scene than one who you see too much of.

So some of them became more important than you'd expected?

Well, we hadn't expected Mr. Humphries to become the main character of the show—he didn't start out with top billing. He was just the kindly mentor for Mr. Lucas (who did have top billing), as opposed to the irascible Mr. Grainger. But every time he spoke, or just walked across the set, he got such a laugh that he was obviously written up more. But even so, he wasn't overused. The danger is overusing somebody.

Were Young Mr. Grace and the porters, Mr. Mash and later Mr. Harman, always intended for the larger roles they have in later episodes, as they appear only intermittently in the early shows?

They grew out of the plot. It was necessary to have a head of the firm, but you didn't know how he was going to turn out until you gave him a couple of pretty nurses and saw where that went. In a comedy you can't keep the humor going all the time without going somewhere else, so to be able to go upstairs to see him dealing with the nurses and his own personal problems—having his pacemaker put in and that sort of thing—was very entertaining. (Of course, the dads like the nurses as well!) The canteen also gave you somewhere else to go, to discuss the world, politics, and the class structure out there, whether you lived in a semidetached house or not. Of course, what nobody ever asked in all the 69 shows was what happened to the store while they were having lunch. Fortunately, nobody ever asked the question.

Trevor Bannister has commented that Mr. Lucas began as the voice of sanity in the store, and that his role diminished as he became as mad as the rest of them.

Yes. We had a slight problem finding a role for him because although he was the new assistant, the youngest assistant, he wasn't clearly that young a man. But he was such a good actor that we wanted him and therefore he did have a large role. But gradually John Inman became a stronger and stronger character, and Mr. Lucas, to a certain extent, diminished. That's what happens in a series.

Were the actors cast to the parts?

The actors were very much cast to be the characters as written. The characters were so easily definable—Mrs. Slocombe was very like my grandmother and uses the same language because she's from the north. They're all based on real-life characters, and the realism of the characters, their believability, was what made it work. They weren't cartoon characters; they were real people that still exist today. Because they were believable, their arguments were believable, and their problems were believable.

How similar were the actors to the characters?

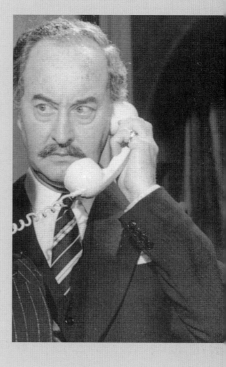

Each [character] was an extension of themselves. They could slip into the role and play it very well, because they could find that character within themselves. Some actors find it hard to find a character, but here I don't think they had to work too hard at it. Arthur Brough played his character to perfection, but he was a gentle man, a kind man, and that came across. Captain Peacock has a normal air of authority—he's a very smart, elegant gentleman. They were very much like the characters off the set.

Were the actors easy to work with?

They were no trouble at all. They relished their parts and were wonderful learners. There were bits which they developed, and as writers we attended every rehearsal, and even up until the night of the show, we would make little changes accordingly. If we saw a drawer sticking or something, we might make Mrs. Slocombe shut it with her bottom.

What about the special effects?

We were rather good, I thought, at inventing special effects—the displays which went wrong. There was a golfer doing a slow golf swing, which would come back and lift her skirt while she's having a serious conversation with somebody. We used to get a lot of laughs out of the special effects. It's really pricking pomposity. The BBC had a marvelous special effects department, and their special effects worked wonderfully. We were their major source of excitement.

Were you ever tempted to write yourself a guest role?

Yes, very tempted, but my partner would never let me. So I was never in the show, though I did the odd 𝖛𝖔𝖎𝖈𝖊-𝖔𝖋𝖋 for it. I think I did an uncredited voice-off as Ted Heath, the ex-prime minister ousted by Mrs. Thatcher, in the one where they went to Ten Downing Street.

But you did appear in Grace and Favour.

Well, that was only because I had the car and knew how to drive it. They were hiring my Rolls, but they decided in the end that they'd have a newer one, which wasn't so rare, but by then they were committed to using me anyway.

From the sixth season onwards, the show's cast was constantly changing.

Well, Arthur Brough, who was always driving people mad in rehearsal, playing musical instruments, tapping glasses, and making music, sadly died. So we brought in as a replacement James Hayter who was 𝖊𝖓𝖌𝖆𝖌𝖊𝖉 as 𝕸𝖗. 𝕶𝖎𝖕𝖑𝖎𝖓𝖌 for the cake 𝖆𝖉𝖛𝖊𝖗𝖙𝖘. But Mr. Kipling's Cakes felt that the indignities he suffered in *Are You Being Served?* took away his authority as Mr. Kipling, and so he resigned from *Are You Being Served?* in favor of doing the adverts.

𝖛𝖔𝖎𝖈𝖊-𝖔𝖋𝖋
voiceover

(to) engage someone
to hire someone

𝕸𝖗. 𝕶𝖎𝖕𝖑𝖎𝖓𝖌
one of Britain's leading manufacturers of dessert cakes and biscuits, a (nonexistent) character brought to life in advertisements

𝖆𝖉𝖛𝖊𝖗𝖙
advertisement

After that we brought in Alfie Bass, but while he was very good, we couldn't do as much with him as we thought we might, although he was a consummately good actor. He thought he needed a bigger part, and we couldn't make the part bigger, so he moved on. Then we replaced him with a similar character, but I think he in turn got a part in a play, and so he left mid-season. Then we got in this lovely old man with a big white beard, who when we auditioned him said his address was the third cardboard box on the left. We all felt so sorry for him that he got the part. But then he went and died. We were jumping in and out of funerals. So after that we went for Mike Berry, who looked as if he might last for some time. The lucky thing is that the writers didn't die, of course, because when the writers die then every character in the show dies!

Did you consider recasting Mr. Lucas when Trevor Bannister left?

No. To keep the realism, you couldn't have another Mr. Lucas—he had to go and somebody else come in. And Mike Berry was rather modern by comparison to the others, which again made him a disruptive influence who would question every managerial decision before being put down by everybody. So we had someone who could be put down.

How did the set contribute to the series?

The set was a simple one of two counters, with the displays to add variety. It was ingenious in that it separated the two groups of people in a small area and provided a playing area—all at very little expense to the BBC. If it had just been the Gentlemen's Department, then there would have been no conflict and no show. The whole thing was based on introducing ladies into a gentlemen's world and arguing as to who was the most important. Should the ladies' display be in the middle or should the gentlemen's? [Everything arose from] the competition between the two, arbitrated by Captain Peacock, with Mr. Rumbold as the final authority—at least until he was undermined by something on the last page of the script.

How was the set designed?

Interestingly enough, when I worked at Simpson's, I was fired by the person in charge of one of the departments I worked in, the display department. She turned up years later at the BBC as a designer, and her first job was designing *Are You Being Served?* But she made the set seem too nice and too smart, and we had to get somebody from a normal shop to make it more down-market. That seemed to be poetic justice.

Was there any reason why the department moved from the first to the fourth floor?

I think that was a slip of the pen. We never kept, as I'm sure a lot of writers would, a wall chart of what floor we were on. And we somehow managed to get to the fourth floor. I know we realized that we'd done that, and having done it, we decided to stay there. Nobody complained.

Why did the series end?

We just found that we'd run out of ideas. The BBC asked us if we wanted to do another series, but I couldn't think of any more ideas. It had come logically to its conclusion, so it just ended there. But I regret that we never got round to the staff outing. We had always thought that at the end of the show, the last show should be the staff outing. Once we talked about going away, and had the slides up and the pictures of going away to the Middle East, to Jeddah, I think, but we never went. The fun was discussing the holiday, I suppose.

How did Grace and Favour actually come about?

Grace and Favour [called *Are You Being Served Again!* in the US] was something which had been at the back of my mind for a long time, [the idea] to move to a country house. David Croft agreed that it would be a good idea at some point to do it, but it took some years to persuade the BBC.

The cast thoroughly enjoyed it, because we lived out in the country while we were doing it, in this lovely house. We gave John Inman a girlfriend, that is, a girl who was very keen on him without realizing that he really was a confirmed bachelor, a mother's boy. We had these hilarious scenes of him waking up in bed with her and phoning his mother to say that he'd gone to bed with the cook—"You need never worry again."

Again we created a family, a complete family surviving with each other and keeping up appearances. I'd like to think that one would quite like to go and live there, because they were obviously having fun. They are basically support-ive of each other. Everybody knows the truth about Captain Peacock's war record, but they'll only mention it in the heat of an argument.

Why did Grace and Favour end after only two seasons? **?**

Things take a while to catch on—[a show] may go out at a time when there's something established on the other side or whatever. It takes a while to build an audience. [With *Are You Being Served?*] we'd built up a dozen shows, and [the BBC] repeated them. When they repeated them, they took off enormously. Suddenly the word got round, and it became a cult [show] and enormously popu-lar. The nice thing about the BBC then was that they were willing to wait and build an audience, so it might start with four or five million, and then rise to six or seven, and then suddenly by the repeats we were getting ten or eleven million.

Grace and Favour had a lot going for it, and a lot of people say they miss it enormously, but it was still building when it ended. The BBC management has changed a lot, and they decided it was very old-fashioned, I think. They wanted alternative comedy, which went on to get much lower figures but was certainly alternative. They never repeated *Grace and Favour*. As repeats helped *Are You Being Served?* enormously, I think they would have done the same for *Grace and Favour*. The audience that watched it loved it—they had to get used to the char-acters being in different surroundings, but the characters were much loved. I think the figures were around six or seven million, which wasn't enough for the

BBC, which works on figures now, not on audience appreciation. They are there to be repeated, and hopefully they will be, but if they do decide to do some more [episodes], the cast aren't going to live for ever, and neither are the writers.

Was it difficult to write Grace and Favour, given that the hierarchy had been removed when the store closed?

Mr. Rumbold worried that his authority had been undermined, so we had to make him the keeper of the purse, so he still had the power to make decisions. Some of the pecking order went, but it was so well established that everybody still knew their place.

We were very much trying to keep it on the same track while moving into another area—happy retirement—but still trying to make money out of what they've been given, whether by keeping chickens, rustling sheep, or just by having guests stay.

What was your favorite episode?

The greatest episode, I think, because it was rather touching at the end, was "A Change Is as Good as a Rest" [in the fifth season of *Are You Being Served?*], in which they decided to run the Toy Department. We went off to the equivalent of FAO Schwarz—Hamleys—and looked at all the toys and bought those we wanted for the show, and made up the show around them. The characters had great arguments over who'd put the lemonade in the doll which went on the potty, and we got lots of fun out of the toys. At the end we had Mr. Grainger playing with the trains, wearing a railwayman's hat. That was very sympathetic and charming.

Do you have plans for other series?

We're going to do another pilot in January 1995. Again, it's a hierarchical thing, set in Eastern Europe, where there's still a lot of the 1920s/1930s aura and outlook on life. And again, the modern world is intruding into something with a long history, which I always find an interesting conflict.

TAPING THE Shows

THE PRODUCTION CYCLE FOR EACH EPISODE OF *Are You Being Served?* was six days, beginning with a "run-through," an informal session during which the actors and all the key personnel sat round a table and quite literally read the script out loud. Any major changes, stemming from objections by the actors to their lines or potential technical difficulties spotted by the makeup, costume, or set departments, were discussed. At some point during the day, the read-through was timed to make sure that the script did not run over or under the allotted half hour.

From that point, the cast moved with the director and producer to the legendary "Acton Hilton" (otherwise known as the BBC Rehearsal Room Facility in North Acton), which is only a short distance from the main BBC Television Centre in Shepherd's Bush, in West London. With its many rehearsal rooms spread over twelve floors, a vast reception area entered through huge revolving doors, and its hotel-like look and feel, this facility soon acquired its apt moniker.

If there was any location filming required, it was usually carried out just prior to the studio rehearsals, normally within a 60-mile radius of London. This made it possible for the cast and camera crews to use BBC Television Centre as a base, and travel to and from there each day, should it be required. Rehearsals normally took place Monday to Friday, with the cast then moving into the studio for the final rehearsal and actual taping, which invariably fell over the course of the weekend. At the beginning of the "Studio Day," the cast rehearsed with the cameras to allow the camera operators to line up their shots and get them

"*We were very close-knit off-screen. I still see Frank, John Inman, Nicholas Smith, and Wendy. We'd always go to the BBC canteen together and sit around the same table or have a drink in the bar. There were no divisions among the group. After a while, we found that we couldn't stomach BBC food much longer. So every Sunday, when we recorded the shows, we all ganged together and brought in a vast picnic. We'd sit down to these wonderful feasts, complete with wine, a* starter, pudding, *the lot. We used to stage our picnic in whoever's dressing room was the biggest. They became legendary around the BBC.*"—Trevor Bannister

in focus. By mid-evening, the studio audience began to arrive and the studio quickly filled up. Audience seating faced the set, with monitors arranged overhead at intervals so the audience could see any action taking place on one of the "sub" sets out of view as well as taped sections of location work. When taped sections were run, the main action on set paused for this to be screened, so that the audience would not lose track of the plot.

Traditionally, a warm-up act was used to get the audience in the right mood for the actual recording, with a barrage of inevitably bad jokes, so that, as someone observed, "whatever follows will be brilliant by comparison." The warm-up person or the production assistant then introduced the actors one by one, and each briefly familiarized the audience with his or her character.

With sitcoms, the policy is largely to try to complete scenes in the same order as they're seen on screen. Almost always, a number of sequences have to be staged two or three times, whether due to human error or otherwise. Hopefully, the audiences continue to find the jokes just as funny for the second, third, or even fourth time around, as the laughter is very important on the soundtrack; there's nothing worse than having to use "canned" laughter.

starter
appetizer before main course of meal

pudding
dessert

"*In one episode [Arthur Brough] was supposed to be a lord and had to wear this toupee. The old bugger used to keep moving it so that every time we looked at him, his toupee would be at a different angle. It was impossible for us to keep a straight face. He was always playing jokes to make us crack up. If there was a scene in the canteen with Mr. Grainger eating spaghetti, you could bet your life that Arthur would suck the spaghetti as noisily as possible.*"—Trevor Bannister

MINDING THE
Script

"We've always had a lot of laughs making the show—not all of them intentional. I remember the time we had to do a retake after I got my tongue in a twist and proclaimed, 'Captain Peacock—are you pee?' The whole studio just folded up in hysterics. Frank Thornton and I only had to look at each other and we'd start laughing again. In all, it took three attempts to redo that scene!"
—Mollie Sugden

"We realized early on that there was no need for any jealousy because I couldn't say lines that Mrs. Slocombe said or vice versa. A line that Captain Peacock speaks was totally written for him. —John Inman

CANNED LAUGHTER WAS ALMOST NEVER USED ON *Are You Being Served?* Funny lines rarely failed to generate gales of laughter. As to whether the lines were often ad-libbed, Clive Parker explains, "The thing about situation comedies is that the writers time the scripts and bring them in word perfect, and really, there isn't that much room for ad-libbing. For elaborating on the jokes, and taking them in new directions, that happens in the rehearsal rooms, so the writers know what the actors want to do with their work beforehand. There just isn't the time or money to be able to afford lengthy ad-libbing sessions in a TV studio, although outtakes are inevitable."

Fans of *Are You Being Served?* often wonder where certain catchphrases such as "I'm free!" came from. "The 'I'm free!' phrase was there all along, as far as I know," recalls Parker. "It was something that happened in department stores. Jeremy Lloyd had worked at one and knew that when one of the shop assistants needed help, he'd ask if a colleague was free to assist, and the traditional reply was 'I'm free!' John homed in on that and took the opportunity to make it his catchphrase, and it became a national pastime to quote it."

There are no records of horrendous mistakes or accidents on the *Are You Being Served?* set, which is surprising, given the show's longevity. There were plenty of scrambled words and phrases, but none of the pratfalls or trip-ups that might be expected. One incident, however, does stand out for Pete Chapman, a camera operator. "We had a shop window dummy that was wearing a Santa

Claus outfit. The special effects department had rigged it up to open its costume as it said 'Yo-ho-ho! Merry Christmas!'" recalls Chapman. "In the script, Mr. Humphries was meant to see [that] it was naked underneath and faint. Well, some of the technicians went down to a rather sordid shop in central London and bought dozens of sex aids and toys, which they put on the dummy, knowing full well that when it opened the cape, John [Inman] would be the one who was face to face with all this stuff. When it came to the take, everyone was sitting there waiting to see his reaction. The dummy opened wide, but everything had gone! The whole lot had been stolen. It was a mystery for the rest of the series as to who had 𝔭𝔦𝔫𝔠𝔥𝔢𝔡 the stuff and who had dared to take it all home. There were one or two suggestions about the BBC Board of Governors, but they're not really repeatable. The strange thing was that, according to rumor, the guy who went to buy all the stuff actually managed to claim it all back on expenses!"

(to) pinch
to steal

"That lot on Are You Being Served? were certainly real professionals. They stuck together, like some sort of family, always clucking round Arthur Brough and Harold Bennett (Young Mr. Grace), because they were so much older than everyone else. They were always checking they were alright, whether they needed a drink, or whatever."
—Pete Chapman, camera operator

"One of the directors insisted that Captain Peacock have a fresh carnation in his buttonhole every week, and this led to a row between the props department and the costume department as to whether that was their or our responsibility. I think someone thought that because Frank [Thornton] took out the flower and sniffed it in one shot, it suddenly became a prop. Things like that used to happen on every series at the BBC. There was once a strike caused by an argument between unions over who got to turn on a studio clock."—Jo Lewis, costumer

DAY TWO of a super Star series

By STAFFORD HILDRED and MICHAEL HELLICAR

BRITAIN'S zaniest shop assistants— the cast of Are You Being Served?— are sitting round a table in a BBC rehearsal room.

It is the first run-through of the script for this week's episode of the top-rated TV series.

The writers have decreed that the limp-wristed Mr. Humphries, played by John Inman, must make a joke about his arch enemy Mrs. Slocombe's underwear.

"The word 'drawers' is typed here," points out Inman.

'Surely Mr. Humphries wouldn't be so common? He'd use a classy word, like 'knickers'.'

The rehearsal stops while cast, writers, director and producer hold a lengthy — and hilarious — debate over which word Mr. Humphries should use.

Everyone agrees that Mr. Humphries would *never* say drawers and the suggestions come thick and fast.

Decision

Daily Star, April 26, 1983

A "Safehouse" Show

The taping of each episode always had to be completed in one straight evening of recording. There was very little opportunity for location recording or extra days for insert shots. That resulted in *Are You Being Served?* amounting to one of the least expensive productions that the BBC made during that period. It was what was technically known as a "safehouse" show, with every season, barring negotiations for the actors' salaries, having the same underlying costs and a regular viewing audience that gave the series a healthy position in the all-important weekly ratings.

BEHIND THE
Camera

THE ACTUAL RECORDING OF THE EPISODES was done as a "three-camera-setup," in which three studio cameras were positioned proportionately in front of the audience. This basically allowed the director to choose from three different angles.

"The director would be up in the control gallery (situated at the end of the studio opposite to the main set, above the top level of the studio seating), watching what the three cameras were relaying to TV monitors spaced out in front of him," explains Chapman. "All he really had to do was call out instructions to the camera operators, telling them to close in on Mr. Humphries or Captain Peacock or whatever, and cover the time it took to set up that shot by using the image from one of the other cameras already in position."

Because of the presence of the live audience, who needed to be kept engaged as much as possible so they would laugh at the appropriate times, the show was generally edited as it was recorded. This was done by switching back and forth between the three cameras. Occasionally editing was done after the show was taped.

According to Chapman, "*Are You Being Served?* was very much a textbook case of how to film a sitcom. There were never any difficult shots which took hours to set up, or anything like that.

Someone I knew who sat in on one recording said it was like going to the theater to see a farce, because the cast worked so well together there were rarely any cases of 𝔠𝔬𝔯𝔭𝔰𝔦𝔫𝔤 or 𝔡𝔯𝔶𝔦𝔫𝔤. It all flowed smoothly, and whereas some sitcoms took the whole evening, a good three hours, to complete, you could practically set your watches to the fact that *Are You Being Served?* would be over and done with in just over an hour."

Jo Lewis, who worked as a costumer for the cast on some of the early episodes, recalls how the initial designs for each character remained practically the same the entire duration of the series.

"It has to be said that the basic look was based on the style of uniform of a certain department store in London. Miss Brahms always had a more stylized, fashionable version of the uniform, compared to Mrs. Slocombe, who was deliberately made to look like a bit of a frump. Wendy [Richard] was in very good shape, and we played on that fact to the hilt and made her as voluptuous as we could. She used to get a hell of a lot of fan mail from men, so the costume department knew they were doing something right. Mollie [Sugden], on the other hand, used to love all the dreadful gear Mrs. Slocombe turned up in. The more blinding a mix of colors, the happier she was. There used to be a joke that you could color code which season was which from the shades of Mollie's wigs. The men basically had suits that were tailored for the actors, making them look as smart as possible."

"The real show stopper," remembers Bill McCabe, "used to be Mr. Humphries' costume for the musical bit [in the special Christmas episodes, which usually ended with elaborate musical numbers on the shop floor]. His costume was always kept under wraps so that even the rest of the cast had as much of a shock as the audience when he appeared. I certainly remember there were one or two comments amongst the rest of the cast about why 'he' always got the most elaborate outfit. But that was so apt for his character, and they couldn't really argue the point."

𝔠𝔬𝔯𝔭𝔰𝔦𝔫𝔤
committing any of a number of stage gaffes, including breaking into laughter, making a mistake in one's lines, spoiling a scene, or forgetting one's lines

𝔡𝔯𝔶𝔦𝔫𝔤
completely forgetting one's lines

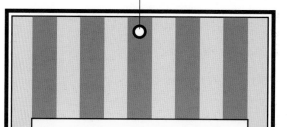

"It was a reliable formula, and everyone knew it worked," says Clive Parker. "I genuinely think it did outlast its life to a certain degree toward the end, but for about ten years, *Are You Being Served?* was like part of the furniture, always waiting there for you every spring when work on the new season started."

Each new season's episodes brought the "family" back together. "Even if there was a different director, the regular cast were always there," says Parker. "I remember that there were never the kind of flare-ups or rows that other programs suffered from during rehearsals. Everyone just got on with the job, determined to get the thing done and make it as funny as possible."

Director Bob Spiers began working on Are You Being Served? at the end of its fifth season, directed the sixth season, and then the ninth. He came to the show as a BBC contract director, fresh from The Goodies. Between seasons he directed a little-known series called Fawlty Towers, written by someone named John Cleese, and directed the Australian version of Are You Being Served? Since Are You Being Served? ended, he's worked on The Comic Strip Presents, Press Gang, and more recently Absolutely Fabulous (which won its second Emmy the week before this interview). He still views Are You Being Served? as a valued part of his career.

Looking back, how do you feel about having worked on Are You Being Served?

I'm very happy to have done [the series] because I think it was a classic bit of old-fashioned British "𝔢𝔫𝔡-𝔬𝔣-𝔱𝔥𝔢-𝔭𝔦𝔢𝔯" humor of a particular kind which we shouldn't lose. It's a bit vulgar, and it's a bit bawdy, and it could be a bit camp, but nevertheless it's good British humor which sits with me very happily alongside all the other stuff I've done. It's a color I'm very glad to have had in my palette.

Do you feel that it's a type of humor that is missing nowadays?

I think they don't quite know how to do it. When you watch the repeats of *Dad's Army* and you then look at shows which are trying to copy it, they don't know how to do it. People like David [Croft] have a certain history which you can't reproduce, and that showed in series like *It Ain't Half Hot, Mum*. It was very skillful, and the jokes were good. Whether you liked them or not, they were good solid jokes.

𝔢𝔫𝔡-𝔬𝔣-𝔱𝔥𝔢-𝔭𝔦𝔢𝔯
off-color or risqué

What were some of the challenges of directing Are You Being Served?

The set was a challenge—whether the lift doors would open. You knew you were onto a winner if they opened, which eight out of ten shows they wouldn't.

So the lift joke grew out of experience on the set?

Yes, I think it came out of quite a lot of experience on set!

Did the set work for or against you, as director?

The set gave you that old-fashioned walk-down, the final scene from the end-of-the-pier show. The stairs gave you a good walk-down, a good entrance for the funny costumes. It's a very obvious setup: You've got Mrs. Slocombe and Miss Brahms on one side, cracking jokes, and then you've got Mr. Humphries and Mr. Lucas on the other side, cracking jokes. Then you've got Captain Peacock in the middle, calling them together, which gave you another setup to crack jokes. Then they'd move on to the canteen and crack jokes. It's so simple that it's difficult, and that's the genius of the program.

How much influence did you have on the content of the scripts? Did you sometimes suggest that the next episode should avoid flashy costumes or too many customers so as to balance the books?

Not really. David was the boss, and he was an experienced producer himself. I'm not a big-budget man, anyway. If I can see something that looks like it's going to be good and we can get away with it financially, then that's what I want to do. David's like that as well. We could change things and suggest different bits of business in rehearsal, and if it was good, he'd say yes. Jeremy [Lloyd] was the same. They were the creators of the program, and it remained their baby throughout.

Sometimes an episode would echo a previous one. When that happened, would you try to make an effort to emphasize the differences or play to the strengths revealed the last time?

Occasionally, because David had written so many shows, something would come up that was a bit similar to something which had gone before, but while it is similar, it's also very different. Very often the plot lines are not the most important thing in these kind of shows—compared with the actors' performances and the dialogue—in determining whether they are essentially funny. And while they may have repeated a bit occasionally, it was always funny.

Did you ever worry the audience wouldn't think it funny?

You never went into an *Are You Being Served?* studio thinking "We're going to have a really ɒuff audience tonight—they're not going to laugh, and we're going to have to come out and put laughs on." People enjoyed it and found it funny.

Would the performances sometimes take you by surprise, lifting a script far beyond your expectations?

Yes, all the time. You'd have a line which on the page wasn't very funny, but once you gave it to John [Inman] he'd make it work. But that's not unusual, because the authors write for these performers and know their strengths— that's what great comic performers are about, that's why they're so valued, that's their talent. They won't make a line into a belly laugh, but they'll turn it into something which is interesting, in a witty way.

ɒuff
substandard, inferior

Do you think the publicity surrounding the casting of someone such as Candy Davis as the secretary was a bonus for the series? [Daughter of a school headmistress and a college professor, Davis ran away from home at age 16 to become a stripper, a story that generated much notice in the press—always accompanied by photos illustrating her ample curves.]

The thing about that character is that you have to look at Young Mr. Grace or Mr. Rumbold to understand the apparent sexism of that part. Candy looked very good and is a very bright lady, and in that situation, that's the combination you go for. I might get the feminists onto me for that, but I don't think that's important—you're in the world of 𝔐𝔠𝔊𝔦𝔩𝔩 𝔭𝔬𝔰𝔱𝔠𝔞𝔯𝔡𝔰, and we'd be mad to lose that.

In the final series, the part of the secretary seemed to become more of a major character in her own right. Was that intended?

I wasn't aware of that happening. She formed a part of those little four-minute scenes in the office, and I can't remember any deliberate ploy to develop her, as there's only so many jokes you can get out of that little segment. The jokes are with John and Mollie, and while you can get some laughs in the office with Mr. Rumbold and the secretary, that's not where the focus lies. So I don't think they'd have done that. Certainly not deliberately.

How did you respond to the gay protests against the series?

𝔐𝔠𝔊𝔦𝔩𝔩 𝔭𝔬𝔰𝔱𝔠𝔞𝔯𝔡𝔰
stylized seaside postcards by an artist named McGill, featuring illustrations of large-breasted women, skinny men, and captions rife with double entendres

I wasn't aware of them, and I don't think I would have taken any notice anyway. I don't think we were doing any damage at all. It was going back to end-of-the-pier stuff, English comic tradition. Those sort of characters had been around for a very long time, and it would be wrong to wipe them out. You have to be very careful about where you land those sort of jokes, and you just have to be responsible. I wouldn't say that we were ever irresponsible.

127

So you believe that the audience shouldn't feel that the character is being laughed at any more than he's laughing at his friends in turn?

Exactly. The fact is that he is his own person, and is acting in the way that he is. Sometimes he's **taking the mickey out of** himself, and sometimes he's not, as we all do.

You worked on the Australian version of the series. How did that come about?

David asked me to go over and do them. We worked from English scripts, and Jeremy did the first series, while I had an Australian writer named Jim Burnett who "Australianized" the shows later on. They did alright—we made 15 of them in all, I think, and they got very big laughs. John [Inman] was extremely good, and we had a very good time in Australia.

Was it something of a culture shock to set up a new cast after working with the long-established team of the original series?

It was more of a culture shock, really, that I did my last *Goodies* on a Friday night for the BBC, which ended my 12-year contract with them, and was sitting on a yacht in Sydney's harbor by Sunday morning. It was the first job that I'd done as a freelancer outside of the BBC, and on that Sunday morning I was thinking, "The freelance life really is better!" That was rather good. In retrospect, having worked in the freelance market for a very long time now, I think I was very naive then, but nevertheless we did get it together. We had a very good set; as good a cast as we could get, because Jeremy had come out and cast them; and the shows were certainly as good as we could make them. It was just a case of getting the Australian crews into the way that I was used to working. And John was brilliant, very supportive and very good.

(to) take the mickey out of
to make fun of

Any interesting adventures while down under?

While out there we went to a very pleasant afternoon party and got quite friendly with some policemen who asked if we'd like to see an Aboriginal area. So they took John, his manager, and myself to this Aboriginal area in

Melbourne where the poverty and alcoholism were quite incredible. The people there were just beside themselves at seeing John. They couldn't believe it. He was fantastic, signing all their autographs, and so on. On the way back we came closer to death than we've ever been. The policemen drove home at 80 mph, missed a turning, and literally nearly killed us! Another time, we'd just finished taping a show, and it's possible that I might just possibly have had one drink over the limit. I made a rather 𝔡𝔬𝔡𝔤𝔶 turn, and suddenly there's the siren, and the police pulled us over. Then I'm telling this young Melbourne policeman that "I'm Bob Spiers from England." John's car had pulled up just behind us, and when he got out, you've never seen a policeman's face change so dramatically. It was Australia, and the people out there don't usually see people like that, so he could not believe that he was seeing Mr. Humphries from *Are You Being Served?* He was so 𝔤𝔬𝔟-𝔰𝔪𝔞𝔠𝔨𝔢𝔡 that he suddenly decided that everything was going to be alright after all.

Was the Australian version a success?

It was funny and it got the laughs, but how successful it was I don't know. I think it had become so successful with the English cast that it had a lot to live up to, though people were really fighting for us. It did well enough to run for two series.

So is there any episode in Are You Being Served? that you remember as a particular favorite?

𝔡𝔬𝔡𝔤𝔶
tricky, risky

𝔤𝔬𝔟-𝔰𝔪𝔞𝔠𝔨𝔢𝔡
shocked or angered
into speechlessness

That's impossible to say. I don't even think about the shows I do in those terms. You just have to come out of the studio feeling that you've done a very good show. Looking at *Fawlty Towers,* I can't think of anything there that I felt particularly proud of—the shows were all very, very hard work, and you hoped that people would laugh, that it would all join up, and that the performances would be good. Amongst what I've done, *Are You Being Served?* fits in as one of the classic, old-fashioned British comedies. I have nothing but extremely fond memories of the show, and I'm very proud to have done it.

Are You Being Served? Not any more reflects Nancy Banks-Smith

Saving Grace

So, Farewell then
Are You Being Served?
In 10 years you never won
A cup or a saucer
Or a suitably inscribed scroll
For your sensitive
* delineation*
Of life on the shop floor.
No-one ever took you to
* Montreux*
For a knees-up
Or accepted an award for you
* saying emotionally*
They owed it all to USDAW.
It seems a shame.
On the other hand
Keith's Mam liked you
And thought Mr Humphries
* was good*
To his mother.

E. J. Thribb-Smith

FOR THOSE of you who have been fiddling about under the lids of your desks for the last 10 years, Are You Being Served? (BBC 1) was a situation comedy about Grace Bros., an unspecified London department store. Personally I rather saw as Pontings, noted for its chill-proof combinations. Grace Bros was so tenacious of life it even outlived its owner, Young Mr Grace, that game if gammy-legged old party, who used to wave his staff on with his walking stick, piping impartially "You're all doing very well!"

And so they were. Particularly Mrs Slocum of Ladies Intimate Apparel and Mr Humphries to whom measuring an inside leg was more of a vocation than an occupation. The characters were so closely related to panto that Mrs Slocum, with her abundant bust and magenta hair, could have been a dame and Mr Humphries a principal boy.

Are You Being Served? was usually spoken of in the same breezy breath as Donald McGill, the saucy postcard man. How easy it is to imagine them all on a staff outing to the seaside, wearing bathing drawers of antique cut. Except, of course, Mr Rumbold's secretary, who was always built on the lines of a roller-coaster and with very much the same effect on the heart.

Are You Being Served? departed this life last night like an old banger, backfiring mild improprieties, bearing

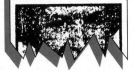

CHANGING EVER SO
Slightly

IN ANY SERIES SPANNING SUCH A LONG PERIOD AS *Are You Being Served?*, there are bound to be changes. For one thing, technology changes.

"Formats of recording things on tape change practically every year," says Pete Chapman. "The editing process went through a revolution at the beginning of the 1980s that offered directors a whole spectrum of choices they never had before. And special effects have progressed in leaps and bounds. But, realistically, with *Are You Being Served?* I don't think anything changed at all in the way the show was actually made. It was a set routine that had a show at the end of the day that everyone loved, and nobody wanted to alter that kind of success. So they left it alone."

"I think that the actors got a bit older, and that's all really," comments Clive Parker. "They turned up for the three months it took to do each batch of episodes, as did the casts of all the other long-running situation comedies, and went through the same old routine. Things have a natural life span, and I think it ran its course."

But Parker recalls how the growth of a dedicated audience altered the show. "One thing that certainly was noticeable was the familiarity of the studio audiences with the characters as the years went by. Initially, there was always the worry of having to stand there and have the actors run through some mini-biography the writers had given them, explaining who they were, etc," he says. "But by about the late 1970s, the thing had become a national, much-loved institution. All you had to do was introduce Frank Thornton by name, and the audience would go wild because they knew the characters back to front. It has to be said that John got the biggest round of applause when he came on, but by that time, it was only to be expected."

STRIKING
The Set

THE FINAL EPISODE OF *ARE YOU BEING SERVED?* was taped in the spring of 1985. "It was sad when it ended because the writers, so I was told, had basically run out of steam," says Bill McCabe. "Sure, there was the odd [episode] that you watched on television and thought it seemed a bit familiar, because they'd had to rework an old plot from a few years earlier, but that happened with *Dad's Army, Steptoe and Son,* you name it, and it happened to them eventually. I think the writers didn't want to fall into a trap of being repetitious for the sake of keeping the show going."

McCabe recalls how the stage crew regretted striking the set for the last time. "I remember when it was all over, the lifts and the **tills** and all the display dummies all went in a **skip**. When the Grace Brothers' sign was seen by some of the riggers, smashed in two as it went off to be burnt, one of the guys said, 'That's like a part of history that's been destroyed.' And I suppose they were right in a way.

till
cash register

skip
large trash container

"*Are You Being Served?*, as far as the behind-the-scenes crew were concerned, had a reputation for being an easy, undemanding show to work on, that had a cast that was easy to get on with, and most importantly of all, knew how to have fun."

The last word is left to costumer Jo Lewis, who went out of her way to get hold of a memento from the series when the final episode had been shot, and the cast and crew had gone home.

"I retrieved Mrs. Slocombe's bright purple wig, and when I got home, I left it on a chair," she recalls. "By the time I'd got back, my cat had gone to sleep on it. Now that's what I call ironic."

I certainly missed my mates at Grace Brothers in the eight-year break between the end of Are You Being Served? and the start of Are You Being Served? Again!, although we often managed to meet socially. Wendy Richard is a special friend. We ring each other quite often and sometimes we go to see saucy films in the afternoon and both die laughing."—John Inman

CHAPTER

3

GRACE
BROS

THE

Episodes

First
SEASON

first broadcast on BBC1 in

19**73**

By Jeremy Lloyd and David Croft
Produced by David Croft

❋❋❋❋❋❋❋❋❋❋❋❋❋❋❋❋❋❋❋❋
Regular Cast

MRS. SLOCOMBE ....*Mollie Sugden*
MR. LUCAS ....*Trevor Bannister*
CAPTAIN PEACOCK ....*Frank Thornton*
MR. HUMPHRIES ....*John Inman*
MR. GRAINGER ....*Arthur Brough*
MR. RUMBOLD ....*Nicholas Smith*
MISS BRAHMS ....*Wendy Richard*

☞ *The order of these billings reflects those used by the BBC at the time. The increasing popularity of John Inman is highlighted by his getting top billing in later episodes.*

☞ *When the producer of a BBC comedy also directs, the BBC tends not to give him or her a separate credit. Hence, David Croft directed every episode of Are You Being Served? unless otherwise indicated.*

❋❋❋❋❋❋❋❋❋❋❋❋❋❋❋❋❋❋❋❋

Episode Ratings

★ ★ ★ ★ *Super*
★ ★ ★ *Jolly good*
★ ★ *Nothing special*
★ *Not up to scratch*

Pilot Episode

★★★★

First transmitted: September 5, 1974 BBC1, UK

MR. MASH	*Larry Martyn*
YOUNG MR. GRACE	*Harold Bennett*
SECRETARY	*Stephanie Gathercole*
CUSTOMER	*Michael Knowles*

For 25 years, the Gentlemen's Ready-to-Wear Department has occupied the first floor of Grace Brothers, a store little changed for decades. But when a reorganization forces the staff to share their space with the Ladies' Department, trouble looms. The junior staff may see advantages to cohabitation, but Mrs. Slocombe and Mr. Grainger are more interested in protecting their interests, and war is soon declared.

☞ *This pilot episode was originally transmitted unexpectedly and without pre-publicity during the 1972 Munich Olympics. The massacre of Israeli athletes by a Palestinian terrorist group led to the cancellation of several days' worth of events, and the BBC ran the pilot in place of planned Olympics coverage. The episode was later repeated at the start of the first series.*

☞ *Michael Knowles played Captain Ashwood in* It Ain't Half Hot, Mum *(Jimmy Perry and David Croft's BBC1 comedy based on a concert party serving in Malaya during the Second World War), and the Honourable Teddy in* You Rang, M'Lord? *(Perry and Croft's parody of Upstairs Downstairs). He also adapted episodes of Dad's Army for BBC Radio and cowrote some episodes of Are You Being Served?*

☞ *Though produced in color, this episode is now believed to survive only in black and white.*

Dear Sexy Knickers

★★★

First transmitted: March 21, 1973 BBC1, UK

THE FORTY-INCH WAIST	*Robert Raglan*
THE TWENTY-EIGHT-INCH INSIDE LEG	*Derek Smith*

Mr. Lucas runs into trouble when Mr. Humphries shows him some of the tricks of the trade, but he gets into even deeper water when his love letter to Miss Brahms is delivered to the wrong person. It seems that Captain Peacock might want to inspect Mrs. Slocombe's underwear, and Miss Brahms might have Mr. Grainger on the carpet.

☞ *Robert Raglan regularly played the Colonel in* Dad's Army, *Jimmy Perry and David Croft's BBC1 sitcom about a Second World War Home Guard unit.*

☞ *The series is still developing here—the Gentlemen's and Ladies' departments aren't supposed to fraternize. Mrs. Slocombe has a soft spot for Mr. Lucas, and Mr. Humphries doesn't even know Miss Brahms' name.*

☞ *Early in the episode Mr. Humphries shows Mr. Lucas how to "knee" a jacket—break the stitches so it will feel roomier. This is a trick Jeremy Lloyd had picked up while working as a junior at Simpson's department store—though he's quick to point out that he would never suggest that any of Simpson's staff ever kneed a jacket.*

not up to scratch
unacceptable

knickers
ladies' underpants

(to call or have) on the carpet
to reprimand

Our Figures Are Slipping

★★★

First transmitted: March 28, 1973 BBC1, UK
Directed by Bernard Thompson

YOUNG MR. GRACE	*Harold Bennett*
SECRETARY	*Stephanie Gathercole*
THE RETURNED GLEN CHECK	*Peter Needham*

When the department's takings drop, Mr. Rumbold hosts a sales conference. But as it's held after the store closes, it's not popular with the staff, and even the threat of getting sacked can't persuade Mr. Lucas to take it seriously. After all, he's got an "unsatisfied virgin" to visit—if he can persuade Miss Brahms to accompany him to the film of the same name.

The Daily Telegraph, March 15, 1973

Television

Promising fun of department store series

By RICHARD LAST

IF the creation of credible funny characters is the essence of television situation comedy, **Are You Being Served?** (B B C·1) could prove a useful addition to the ranks.

Originally shown as a "Comedy Playhouse" pilot, last night's first episode returns to the screen with enhanced status as the forerunner of a full-blown series.

The scene is an old-established and slightly decaying department store, which inevitably brings a train of visual and verbal jokes about [illegible] troub[illegible]

Camping In
★★★★

First transmitted: April 4, 1973 BBC1, UK

MR. MASH	Larry Martyn
SCOT	James Copeland
THE 38C CUP	Anita Richardson
THE LARGE BRIM WITH FRUIT	Pamela Manson
SECRETARY	Stephanie Gathercole
THE MAN WITH THE LARGE BRA	David Rowlands
THE LEATHERETTE GLOVES	Colin Bean

An unexpected transport strike leaves the staff of Grace Brothers stranded, so Young Mr. Grace suggests that they spend the night together. Tents are provided, though Mr. Lucas finds it difficult to keep his erect, and Miss Brahms refuses to leave Captain Peacock's bed, forcing him to kip with Mr. Rumbold. The camaraderie of wartime builds around the "old campfire," but Mr. Humphries is the only member of staff who really feels at home in a row of tents.

☞ *Colin Bean played Private Sponge, a regular background character in Dad's Army.*

☞ *For once, a mistake makes it into the final episode—Captain Peacock greets Miss Brahms as "Missus Brahms."*

☞ *The TV critic of the Morning Star, the newspaper of the Communist Party of Great Britain, always critical of Are You Being Served? on political grounds, commented about this episode that the studio audience guffawed at dropped trousers and collapsing beds as if they'd never seen such things before; later the paper dismissed the "tediously offensive" performance of John Inman.*

His and Hers
★★★★

First transmitted: April 11, 1973 BBC1, UK

MISS FRENCH	Joanna Lumley
MR. MASH	Larry Martyn
FIRST CUSTOMER	Margaret Flint
SECOND CUSTOMER	Evan Ross

The glamourous representative of the "His and Hers" perfume company arrives in the department and sets up shop in the no-man's-land between the Ladies' and Gents' counters. Her arrival causes stirrings in the trouser department, and she makes an immediate impression on Captain Peacock and Mr. Lucas. But Mrs. Slocombe and Mr. Grainger are shocked to discover she's giving it away—in the form of promotional ties and stockings. With their commissions threatened, they unite to turn their fire upon a common enemy.

☞ *Joanna Lumley, later to play Purdey in The New Avengers, Sapphire in Sapphire and Steel, and Patsy Stone in Absolutely Fabulous, also appears in "German Week," the sixth episode of the third series. Not so coincidentally, she is also the ex-wife of the creator of Are You Being Served?, Jeremy Lloyd.*

(to) kip
to (go to) sleep

get into bed with
to join up with, become partners with

Diamonds Are a Man's Best Friend
★★★

First transmitted: April 18, 1973 BBC1, UK

MR. HUMPHRIES' CUSTOMER	Elizabeth Larner
MR. MASH	Larry Martyn
YOUNG MR. GRACE	Harold Bennett
WEALTHY CUSTOMER	Hilary Pritchard
SECRETARY	Stephanie Gathercole
THE OUTSIZE DRESS	Janet Davies
MR. HUMPHRIES' FRIEND	Vicki Woolf

When a customer offers a 100-pound reward for the return of a missing diamond, the staff reveal some shady sides to their characters. Conspiracies abound, and Mr. Grainger is the only one not to get into bed with his colleagues, as they search for the gem amid the debris left when Mr. Mash mistreats a jeweled dress.

☞ *Elizabeth Larner played Ammonia in Up Pompeii!, the innuendo-laden comedy produced by David Croft and starring Frankie Howard.*

☞ *Janet Davies played Mrs. Pike in Dad's Army.*

Dad's Army man hopes there's fun in store

THE road towards original TV comedy becomes more and more stony.

Not the most envious of jobs is held by Duncan Wood at the B.B.C. who has to find laughs which will stretch across something like a thousand hours a year.

Next month he will find, he hopes, a new success with "Are You Being Served?"—a spin-off series

LONG LIST

Like "Dad's Army," it brings together many different characters—all the way from the head of the ladies' department to the underlings in other areas of the store.

It will be a show without stars but with a long list of character actors—like Trevor Bannister, Frank Thornton,

Mollie Sugden, and John Inman.

And it would seem, if "Dad's Army" is anything to go by, a much better bet for a long run with quiet humour than you get from the straight and noisier comedians.

Croft, a past-master at the game of devising this type of almost under-played comedy, tells me: "Once we were known as a nation of shop keepers.

"All right, in a way we shall be identifying with that past. It is a very close look at a very small world in which everybody has his place.

"But it is a world we all come up against, buying the underpants or a cigarette case, without the tainted idea of the curious relationship which exists behind the scenes.

"TV comedy seems to be swinging away from the outrageous and back to the safe situation with which Mrs. Mary Whitehouse will find no quarrel . . ."

Daily Express, February 10, 1973

Second SEASON

first broadcast on BBC1 in

19 74

By Jeremy Lloyd and David Croft
*Produced by Harold Snoad; executive producer,
David Croft*

✳✳✳✳✳✳✳✳✳✳✳✳✳✳✳✳✳✳✳✳✳✳✳

Regular Cast

MRS. SLOCOMBE .... *Mollie Sugden*

MR. LUCAS .... *Trevor Bannister*

CAPTAIN PEACOCK .... *Frank Thornton*

MR. HUMPHRIES .... *John Inman*

MR. GRAINGER .... *Arthur Brough*

MR. RUMBOLD .... *Nicholas Smith*

MISS BRAHMS .... *Wendy Richard*

✳✳✳✳✳✳✳✳✳✳✳✳✳✳✳✳✳✳✳✳✳✳✳

Episode Ratings

★★★★ *Super*

★★★ *Jolly good*

★★ *Nothing special*

★ *Not up to scratch*

The Clock
★ ★ ★

First transmitted: March 14, 1974 BBC1, UK

MR. MASH	Larry Martyn
YOUNG MR. GRACE	Harold Bennett
THE CHECK JACKET	John Ringham
THE BRIDAL VEIL	Dorothy Wayne
MRS. GRAINGER	Pearl Hackney
ELSIE	Hilda Fenemore
THE TRIO	Avril Fane, Barbara and Dorothy Laynes

Mrs. Slocombe gets quite excited when Mr. Mash gives her an electrified cat as a sales aid, but still mucks in when it comes to discussing Mr. Grainger's birthday dinner. He's served Grace Brothers faithfully for 37 years and fears he may be forced to retire. When he's summoned to Mr. Rumbold's office and hears the ticking of his retirement cuckoo clock, it doesn't do much for his ticker.

☞ *New producer Harold Snoad went on to produce* Keeping Up Appearances.

☞ *Beachy Head, where Mrs. Slocombe suggests the Bridal Veil go for her honeymoon, is a cliff on the south coast of Britain notorious for being a suicide spot.*

☞ *This was the first appearance of Elsie, the cleaner played by Hilda Fenemore.*

Cold Comfort
★ ★ ★ ★

First transmitted: March 21, 1974 BBC1, UK

By Jeremy Lloyd, David Croft, and Michael Knowles

MR. MASH	Larry Martyn
YOUNG MR. GRACE	Harold Bennett
ELSIE	Hilda Fenemore
GLADYS	Helen Lambert
FOOTWEAR	Robert Hill
THE LARGE HAT	Carolyn Hudson
THE FUR GLOVES	John Baker

The management of Grace Brothers is quick to respond to the government's plea to conserve the nation's dwindling fuel stocks—by turning the heating off. The staff greet the news very coldly— but they could hardly do otherwise as the temperature drops. Mr. Rumbold may be sitting pretty in his nice warm office, but only the store's stock and the staff's own ingenuity can save them from a frozen end.

☞ *This episode was inspired in part by the miners' strike of winter 1974, which led to power cuts, a three-day work week, and (eventually) the fall of the Conservative government. By the time the episode was transmitted, however, the government had been replaced and the strike brought to an end.*

The Think Tank
★ ★ ★

First transmitted: March 28, 1974 BBC1, UK

MR. MASH	Larry Martyn
YOUNG MR. GRACE	Harold Bennett

In an attempt to preserve the modesty of his female charges, Mr. Rumbold orders Mr. Mash to put petticoats on the female dummies before washing them, yet finds he doesn't like the results. But with sales falling, this is the least of his problems. So he pounces on Captain Peacock's suggestion that they hold a think tank, where they decide that a fashion show might pull in the customers. Young Mr. Grace refuses to hire models, so the staff are forced to put on the show themselves.

think tank
a gathering of (supposedly) intelligent people who compare ideas on a topic and then come up with a plan on how to proceed

Big Brother
★★★★

First transmitted: April 4, 1974 BBC1, UK

By Jeremy Lloyd, David Croft, and Michael Knowles

MR. MASH	*Larry Martyn*
DR. WAINWRIGHT	*Robert Raglan*
MR. CLEGG	*Donald Morley*
SECRETARY	*Stephanie Reeve*
UNDERWEAR CUSTOMER	*Joyce Cummings*
SCARF CUSTOMER	*Stella Kembell*

Someone's been **lifting** Mrs. Slocombe's skirts, and even Mr. Humphries has had a hand rifle through his drawers. Shoplifting strikes Grace Brothers, so Mr. Rumbold installs closed circuit television and calls in a security specialist. Mrs. Slocombe submits to a handbag check, but Mr. Humphries is reluctant to reveal the bulge in his pocket. While the staff succumb to the limelight for a while, they soon tire of surveillance. When Mrs. Slocombe's bust (on which a hat is displayed) brings down Mr. Clegg, they decide to exploit Mr. Rumbold's hypochondria.

☞ *Donald Morley later played Mrs. Slocombe's errant husband in Grace and Favour.*

☞ *Regular Customer: Robert Raglan wanted the Forty-Inch Waist in "Dear Sexy Knickers."*

Hoorah for the Holidays
★★

First transmitted: April 11, 1974 BBC1, UK

MR. MASH	*Larry Martyn*
YOUNG MR. GRACE	*Harold Bennett*
THE MADE-TO-MEASURE CUSTOMER	*John Clegg*
THE DRESSING GOWN CUSTOMER	*Stuart Sherwin*
IRISH CUSTOMER	*Helen Dorward*

Mr. Mash is sticking some juice into Mrs. Slocombe's corsets, and Mr. Lucas is squeezing a customer into his trousers while **tearing him off a strip**. The major concern, though, is that plans for redecorating threaten the staff's freedom to take their holidays when they choose, as Young Mr. Grace wants to close the store while it's being rebuilt. The staff revolt but are mollified when Young Mr. Grace offers to pay for their holidays—until they learn what the options are.

☞ *John Clegg played 'La-De-Dah' Gunner Graham in It Ain't Half Hot, Mum and returns to Grace Brothers in "Wedding Bells."*

☞ *The staff do go on holiday together in the Are You Being Served? film.*

(to) lift
to steal

(to) tear him off a strip
to criticize, probably derived from the military, referring to demotion (removing an officer's stripes)

Third SEASON

first broadcast on BBC1 in

19 75

By Jeremy Lloyd and David Croft
Produced by David Croft

Regular Cast

MRS. SLOCOMBE	Mollie Sugden
MR. LUCAS	Trevor Bannister
CAPTAIN PEACOCK	Frank Thornton
MR. HUMPHRIES	John Inman
MR. GRAINGER	Arthur Brough
MR. RUMBOLD	Nicholas Smith
MISS BRAHMS	Wendy Richard
MR. MASH	Larry Martyn
YOUNG MR. GRACE	Harold Bennett

Episode Ratings

★★★★ *Super*

★★★ *Jolly good*

★★ *Nothing special*

★ *Not up to scratch*

The Hand of Fate
★★★

First transmitted: February 27, 1975 BBC1, UK

MR. KATO ....*Eric Young*
MISS AINSWORTH ....*Nina Francis*
LADY CUSTOMER ....*Therese McMurray*

A rumor is floating around that there will be a vacancy on the board of directors of Grace Brothers, and everyone wonders about their chances of promotion as Mr. Rumbold prepares to ascend the chain of command. Mr. Humphries takes his colleagues by the hand and reveals his skill as a fortune teller. But he's not the only clairvoyant on the staff: Young Mr. Grace has been seeking other advice, namely, that of his secretary, who reads the message in the tea leaves cautioning Young Mr. Grace to beware of a big-eared bald-headed man.

Coffee Morning
★★★★

First transmitted: March 6, 1975 BBC1, UK

MISS AINSWORTH ....*Nina Francis*

All the staff object when Captain Peacock decides to monitor their coffee breaks, but it's Mr. Grainger who drops himself in it when he flushes away five minutes of the firm's time in the little boys' room. "One out, all out," cries Mr. Mash as he leads the staff in revolt—but he sends them in a direction they find revolting and which leads to a Pyrrhic victory when Captain Peacock allows them to take their coffee breaks—but only on the floor, not in the canteen.

Up Captain Peacock
★★★

First transmitted: March 13, 1975 BBC1, UK

THE FORTY MATERNITY ....*Donald Hewlett*
THE BOLD CHECK ....*Michael Knowles*
THE CLIP-ON BOW ....*Jeffrey Segal*
THE CAPTAIN'S FANCY ....*Maureen Lane*

After 20 years in the service of Grace Brothers, Captain Peacock is at last sent up—up the chain of command, that is, with promotion to a senior position. This earns him the privileges of rank—among them the key to the executive toilet and admission to the executive dining room. But his delight enrages Mr. Grainger, and his complaint to the Works' Inspector ensures these privileges prove short lived.

☞ *Donald Hewlett and Michael Knowles had already formed a partnership as Colonel Reynolds and Captain Ashwood in It Ain't Half Hot, Mum, and would later work together in You Rang, M'Lord? (where they played brothers); in the BBC radio series Anything Legal; and in another Jeremy Lloyd/David Croft sitcom, Come Back, Mrs. Noah, where they played the crew of a spacecraft on which Mollie Sugden's title character became stranded.*

(to) drop oneself in it
to get oneself into trouble

Cold Store

★★

First transmitted: March 20, 1975 BBC1, UK

DAPHNE ....*Hilda Fenemore*
THE BLUE ALTERATION ....*Ann Sydney*
SISTER ....*Joy Allen*
THE FAWN TROUSERS ....*Gordon Peters*
...........................*Pamela Cundell*
...................................*Bill Martin*

As the staff struggle to cope with seasonal illnesses, Mr. Lucas schemes to get the day off so he can spend it with a girlfriend.

☞ *How odd…Hilda Fenemore's character used to be called Elsie, not Daphne. And later on, of course, she becomes Ivy.*

Wedding Bells

★★★

First transmitted: March 27, 1975 BBC1, UK

MISS ROBINSON ....*Sandra Clark*
THE SMALL HANDICAP ....*John Clegg*
THE TROUSERS ....*Jay Denyer*

Mrs. Slocombe is driven to the verge of resignation when Mr. Mash puts saucy slogans on her knickers, but reconsiders when she hears that Young Mr. Grace plans to marry one of his staff. When she's called to his office, her colleagues join her in jumping to conclusions and try to ingratiate themselves with their boss-to-be. But Mrs. Slocombe's not the only woman on Grace Brothers' staff, and thoughts of the girls of the Caribbean give Young Mr. Grace second thoughts about marriage, anyway.

☞ *Regular Customer: John Clegg was the Made-to-Measure Customer back in "Hoorah for the Holidays."*

German Week

★★★

First transmitted: April 3, 1975 BBC1, UK

MISS THORPE ....*Moira Foot*
GERMAN CUSTOMERS
...............*Ernst Ulman, Joanna Lumley*
THE LADY FOR THE LADIES
...........................*Anita Richardson*

Grace Brothers stages a special theme week in which they try to promote German goods. But the staff find themselves inundated with German customers seeking British goods, and things go from bad to worse when Mrs. Slocombe samples the German wine.

☞ *Repeat Business: Joanna Lumley also appears in "His and Hers," and Anita Richardson was the 38C Cup in "Camping In."*

Shoulder to Shoulder

★ ★ ★

First transmitted: April 10, 1975 BBC1, UK
By David Croft, Jeremy Lloyd,
and Michael Knowles
Directed by Ray Butt

THE HONEYMOON COUPLE
............*Jonathan Cecil, Hilary Pritchard*
MISS THORPE ....*Moira Foot*
THE RETURNED WIG ....*Kate Brown*

Young Mr. Grace decides to redecorate the ladies' counter, so Mrs. Slocombe and Miss Brahms have to share a counter with the men while the work is carried out.

☞ *Regular Customer: Hilary Pritchard was the customer who lost her diamond in "Diamonds Are a Man's Best Friend."*

New Look

★ ★

First transmitted: April 17, 1975 BBC1, UK
By David Croft, Jeremy Lloyd, and Michael Knowles
Directed by Ray Butt

MISS THORPE ....*Moira Foot*
THE GENT FOR THE GENTS ...*Felix Bowness*

A general discussion among the staff results in the store getting a Great Gatsby makeover—to musical accompaniment.

☞ *Felix Bowness played jockey Fred Quilley in Jimmy Perry and David Croft's holiday camp sitcom Hi-de-Hi!*

☞ *New Look was the name of a variety series for which Jeremy Lloyd wrote in the 1950s.*

Christmas Crackers

★ ★

First transmitted: December 24, 1975 BBC1, UK
Directed by Ray Butt

WAITRESS ....*Doremy Vernon*

The staff of Grace Brothers seek ways to boost Christmas sales, but they are not amused when Young Mr. Grace decides that they should wear fancy dress. Miss Brahms proves a convincing fairy, and Mr. Lucas straps his leg up as Long John Silver. Mr. Grainger ends up with egg on his face as Humpty Dumpty, and Mrs. Slocombe proves off-target as Robin Hood, leaving Mr. Mash less than impressed.

☞ *This was Doremy Vernon's first appearance. In later seasons, she appears regularly as the canteen manageress.*

Christmas crackers
novelty items sold during the holiday season; fancily wrapped cardboard cylinders that are pulled from both ends, making a snapping or "cracking" sound when the wrapping tears off and revealing toys, candy, or other small trinkets inside; also, rhyming slang for knackers, or testicles

Fourth SEASON

first broadcast on BBC1 in

19**76**

By Jeremy Lloyd and David Croft
Produced by David Croft; directed by Ray Butt

✻✻✻✻✻✻✻✻✻✻✻✻✻✻✻✻✻✻✻

Regular Cast

MRS. SLOCOMBE	Mollie Sugden
MR. LUCAS	Trevor Bannister
CAPTAIN PEACOCK	Frank Thornton
MR. HUMPHRIES	John Inman
MISS BRAHMS	Wendy Richard
MR. GRAINGER	Arthur Brough
MR. RUMBOLD	Nicholas Smith
YOUNG MR. GRACE	Harold Bennett

✻✻✻✻✻✻✻✻✻✻✻✻✻✻✻✻✻✻✻

Episode Ratings

★★★★ *Super*
★★★ *Jolly good*
★★ *Nothing special*
★ *Not up to scratch*

No Sale
★ ★ ★ ★

First transmitted: April 8, 1976 BBC1, UK

IVY	Hilda Fenemore
THE CHECK SUIT	John Bardon
THE LARGE GLOVES	Stuart Sherwin
THE WEDDING HAT	Hilary Pritchard
HUSBAND	Gordon Peters
WIFE	Anne Cunningham
THE RAINCOAT IN THE WINDOW	Reg Dixon

Young Mr. Grace decides to open the store at 8:30 a.m. so the public can shop on their way to work. But the staff prefer to stay in bed in the morning and decide to sabotage the idea. They put all their energy into discouraging the customers, and the success of this effort becomes evident in their sales.

☞ *Repeat Business: Having been one of the honeymoon couple in "Shoulder to Shoulder," Hilary Pritchard now wants a wedding hat. And Gordon Peters is also making a return to the store.*

Top Hat and Tails
★ ★ ★

First transmitted: April 15, 1976 BBC1, UK
Dance staged by Frances Pidgeon

MR. HARMAN	Arthur English
MR. LUDLOW	Peter Greene

The Ladies' and Gents' departments of Grace Brothers form a team to enter the inter-store ballroom dancing competition. Mr. Humphries calls upon his theatrical background to train the team, but he runs into difficulty because of the imbalance of the sexes. Once the costumes provided by the Dress Hire Department prove inadequate, he realizes that only a dummy would volunteer for job of dancer—and sets out to recruit one.

Forward Mr. Grainger
★ ★ ★ ★

First transmitted: April 22, 1976 BBC1, UK

SECRETARY	Isabella Rye

When Mr. Rumbold is sent on a sales and management course for a month, Mr. Grainger is assigned to take his place, much to the dismay of Captain Peacock. Mr. Humphries takes over Mr. Grainger's tape measure, and Mr. Grainger takes over the executive drinks trolley. The staff wonder whether they should take advantage of Mr. Grainger's good nature, only to discover that he doesn't have one when he fires Mrs. Slocombe.

Fire Practice
★ ★ ★ ★

First transmitted: April 29, 1976 BBC1, UK

MR. HARMAN	Arthur English
INTERPRETER	Ahmed Khalil
EMIR	Ahmed Osman
HEAD WIFE	Melody Urquhart
FIREMAN	Hamish Roughead
CHIEF FIREMAN	Ken Barker

A surprise fire drill leaves Mr. Rumbold terribly nervous, but this comes as no surprise to the staff. On the other hand, the arrival of an Arab sheik who insists that no man can touch his wives and live but who offers to pay for his goods with spare wives does come as a shock. The resultant chaos shows that Grace Brothers' fire precautions leave a lot to be desired. So Mr. Harman helps out training the staff in fire preparedness, and a fireman gives Mr. Humphries a lift.

Fifty Years On

★ ★ ★

First transmitted: May 5, 1976 BBC1, UK

MR. HARMAN	Arthur English
CLAUDE	Tony Sympson
MRS. CLAUDE	Mavis Pugh
MR. GRACE'S SECRETARY	Penny Irving
THE SIX-POUND FOX	Diana Lambert

Mrs. Slocombe has been dropping hints about her birthday all over the place, so when Miss Brahms deduces that she'll be 50, the rest of the staff decide to organize an appropriate celebration. The cake proves to be something of a **bloomer**, but not nearly so great a one as Miss Brahms' **maths**.

☞ *Diana Lambert later played Mrs. Peacock—who, coincidentally, makes her first appearance (played by Diana King) in the following episode.*

☞ *Penny Irving makes her first appearance as Mr. Grace's secretary, later to be named Miss Bakewell and then Miss Nicholson. Penny Irving is an ex-***Page Three Girl***.*

Oh What a Tangled Web

★ ★ ★

First transmitted: May 12, 1976 BBC1, UK

MR. HARMAN	Arthur English
MRS. PEACOCK	Diana King
MONICA HAZLEWOOD	Melita Manger
MR. GRACE'S SECRETARY	Penny Irving
MR. HAZLEWOOD	Michael Stainton

Rumors fly when Captain Peacock gets too friendly with Mr. Rumbold's secretary at the Christmas party, and events run out of control when it seems the "lovers" might have spent the night together. Mrs. Peacock invades the store, and Young Mr. Grace decides to convene a board of inquiry. Mr. Harman is relentless in his pursuit of the truth, and the Peacocks stick together—perhaps to the captain's regret.

☞ *The cast of Are You Being Served? appeared in "Seaside Special," a summer variety show broadcast from holiday resort theaters and hosted by Ken Dodd, on June 19th, 1976.*

The Father Christmas Affair

★ ★ ★

First transmitted: December 24, 1976
Dance staged by Michele Hardy

MR. HARMAN	Arthur English
THE PLASTIC UMBRELLA	Jeanne Mockford
THE COOK	Doremy Vernon
MISS BAKEWELL	Penny Irving
THE BOY	Donald Waugh

A substantial bonus is to be given to the successful candidate for the post of Grace Brothers' Father Christmas, and money, as usual, brings out the staff's worst competitive instincts. Sex discrimination is clearly forbidden, so Mother Christmas, Miss Christmas, and Principal Boy Christmas join the lineup before Young Mr. Grace decides he doesn't believe in Santa Claus.

☞ *Jeanne Mockford played Senna the Soothsayer in Up Pompeii!*

☞ *Job Change: Doremy Vernon was a waitress a year ago; now she's become the cook!*

☞ *The Sex Discrimination Act, ensuring equal treatment at work, was passed the year before this episode was made.*

bloomer
embarrassing mistake

maths
mathematics

Page Three Girl
a model who has appeared in topless pin-ups on page three of Britain's tabloid newspapers

Fifth SEASON

first broadcast on BBC1 in

19**77**

By Jeremy Lloyd and David Croft
Produced by David Croft

Regular Cast

MRS. SLOCOMBE ....Mollie Sugden
MR. LUCAS ....Trevor Bannister
CAPTAIN PEACOCK ....Frank Thornton
MR. HUMPHRIES ....John Inman
MISS BRAHMS ....Wendy Richard
MR. GRAINGER ....Arthur Brough
MR. RUMBOLD ....Nicholas Smith
YOUNG MR. GRACE ....Harold Bennett
MR. HARMAN ....Arthur English

Episode Ratings

★ ★ ★ ★ *Super*
★ ★ ★ *Jolly good*
★ ★ *Nothing special*
★ *Not up to scratch*

Mrs. Slocombe Expects
★ ★ ★

First transmitted: February 25, 1977 BBC1, UK
Directed by Ray Butt

The staff have kittens when Mrs. Slocombe announces she's expecting a happy event, but it's merely her pussy that's with child—not that this saves them any bother in the long run, as she's afraid to leave Tiddles unattended. She decides to set up a nursery in the Ladies' Fitting Room, right in the middle of Mr. Rumbold's sales drive.

A Change Is as Good as a Rest
★ ★ ★ ★

First transmitted: March 4, 1977 BBC1, UK
Directed by Ray Butt

MISS BAKEWELL ....*Penny Irving*
THE RED INDIAN FATHER ....*Terry Duggan*
THE BRIDAL DOLL ....*Jacquie Cook*

The staff are outraged when alterations in Grace Brothers' staffing arrangements lead to changes in their routine. But Young Mr. Grace's decision to transfer the staff of Gents' and Ladies' Ready-to-Wear to the Toy Department proves quite a success.

☞ *This is Jeremy Lloyd's favorite episode.*

Founder's Day
★ ★ ★

First transmitted: March 11, 1977 BBC1, UK
Directed by Ray Butt

THE TWO FUR COATS ....*Tim Barrett*
THE TOP-POCKET HANDKERCHIEF
..................................*Bill Martin*
THE FRENCH UNDERWEAR
...........................*Carole Rousseau*
MISS BAKEWELL ....*Penny Irving*
MISS 38-22-36 ....*Jenny Kenna*

The staff decide to mark Young Mr. Grace's eightieth birthday with a show celebrating the greatest moments of his life.

The Old Order Changes
★ ★ ★

First transmitted: March 18, 1977 BBC1, UK
Directed by Ray Butt

THE AFRO PANTS ....*Jeffrey Holland*
CYNTHIA ....*Bernice Adams*

Young Mr. Grace returns from the United States with some startling new ideas, and soon an all-new Grace Brothers bids the customers welcome with a barrage of new sales techniques.

☞ *Jeffrey Holland played camp comic Spike Dixon in Hi-de-Hi! and butler James Twelvetrees in You Rang, M'Lord?*

Takeover
★ ★

First transmitted: March 25, 1977 BBC1, UK
Directed by Ray Butt

LADY WEEBLE ABLESMITH ......*Mavis Pugh*
HENRY GRANT HOPKINS ......*Donald Bisset*
MISS BAKEWELL ....*Penny Irving*

Grace Brothers' foundations tremble—not to mention Ladies' Underwear—as the Ladies' and Gents' fashion departments are enlisted to defeat a takeover bid.

Goodbye Mr. Grainger
★ ★ ★

First transmitted: April 1, 1977 BBC1, UK
Directed by Ray Butt

THE CORSET CUSTOMER ....*Peggy Ashby*

Mr. Grainger has never been the best natured of colleagues, but recently he's become so bad-tempered that the rest of the staff demand his resignation, leaving questions as to whether his days at Grace Brothers are numbered.

It Pays to Advertise
★ ★ ★ ★

First transmitted: April 8, 1977 BBC1, UK
Directed by Bob Spiers

THE TEN-POUND PERFUME ....*Ferdy Mayne*
THE PORTER ....*Freddie Wiles*
MISS BAKEWELL ....*Penny Irving*
MR. CRAWFORD ....*Raymond Bowers*

Young Mr. Grace decides to advertise in the local cinemas. Fame beckons for the staff of Grace Brothers, but Mr. Grace may have been less than wise when he tried to save money by employing them.

☞ *Ferdy Mayne later moved to America, where he had a semiregular role as Albert Grand in Cagney and Lacey.*

☞ *This is the first episode directed by Bob Spiers.*

Sixth
SEASON

first broadcast on BBC1 in
19**78**

By Jeremy Lloyd and David Croft
Produced by David Croft; directed by Bob Spiers

Regular Cast

MRS. SLOCOMBE	Mollie Sugden
MR. HUMPHRIES	John Inman
MR. LUCAS	Trevor Bannister
CAPTAIN PEACOCK	Frank Thornton
MISS BRAHMS	Wendy Richard
MR. TEBBS	James Hayter
MR. RUMBOLD	Nicholas Smith
YOUNG MR. GRACE	Harold Bennett
MR. HARMAN	Arthur English
MISS BAKEWELL	Penny Irving
NURSE	Vivienne Johnson

Episode Ratings

★★★★ *Super*
★★★ *Jolly good*
★★ *Nothing special*
★ *Not up to scratch*

By Appointment
★ ★ ★

First transmitted: November 15, 1978 BBC1, UK

IVY . . . . *Hilda Fenemore*

LADY CUSTOMER . . . . *Joy Harrington*

Mr. Tebbs is transferred to Gents' Out-fitting from Bathrooms and Beddings as a flutter grips the store. It seems there's to be a **royal walkabout** near Grace Brothers, and if time permits, the royal party may visit the store. The staff prepare their departments to receive the royal presence.

☞ *Joy Harrington also appeared earlier that same evening on BBC1 in the children's serial The Moon Stallion alongside Sarah Sutton and Caroline Goodall (the future stars of Doctor Who and Schindler's List, respectively).*

🇬🇧

royal walkabout
a public stroll taken by the monarch or other member of the Royal Family

The Club
★ ★ ★

First transmitted: November 22, 1978 BBC1, UK

ROGER'S MASTER . . . . *Raymond Bowers*

ROGER'S MISTRESS . . . . *Mavis Pugh*

FLEXIBRA CUSTOMERS

. . . . *Dominique Don, Tony Brothers*

The staff find a reason to spend time in the cellar when Young Mr. Grace gives his workers a room in which to form a social club. To save money, they decide to decorate it themselves.

☞ *Mavis Pugh had previously played Lady Weeble Ablesmith in Takeover.*

Do You Take This Man?
★ ★ ★ ★

First transmitted: November 29, 1978 BBC1, UK

WENDEL P. CLARK . . . . *Norman Mitchell*

MR. TOMIADES . . . . *Gorden Kaye*

THE MATCHING PANTALOONS

. . . . *Felix Bowness*

GREEK BAND LEADER . . . . *Stellios Chiotis*

Mrs. Slocombe finally gets her man, a bouzouki player in a Greek restaurant. Her colleagues set about organizing a wedding reception, but when the fellow's brother comes to call, she realizes how little she knows about his family—particularly the female members.

☞ *Gorden Kaye later played Rene Artois in 'Allo, 'Allo for David Croft, and a TV presenter in Mollie Sugden's other vehicle, Come Back, Mrs. Noah.*

☞ *Felix Bowness was the Gent for the Gents in "New Look."*

Shedding the Load
★ ★ ★

First transmitted: December 6, 1978 BBC1, UK

REGULAR CAST ONLY

Sales figures are down, profits are lower. A gloomy Young Mr. Grace decides to make staff cutbacks. If someone has to go, then someone must choose who.

A Bliss Girl
★ ★ ★

First transmitted: December 13, 1978 BBC1, UK

LADY CUSTOMER . . . . *Jan Holden*

TYPIST . . . . *Bernice Adams*

A perfume display arrives from Bliss but with no one to sell the product. Mrs. Slocombe sees no percentage in selling perfume when she'll lose her commission on the clothes, so to help out, Mr. Humphries agrees to sell perfume for a day.

Happy Returns
★ ★ ★ ★

First transmitted: December 26, 1978 BBC1, UK

FAIRY PRINCE . . . . *Michael Halsey*

WAITRESS . . . . *Doremy Vernon*

It's Young Mr. Grace's birthday. After the customary free lunch in the canteen, the staff set about organizing a cabaret for his birthday party.

Seventh SEASON

first broadcast on BBC1 in

19**79**

By Jeremy Lloyd and David Croft
Produced by David Croft

✻✻✻✻✻✻✻✻✻✻✻✻✻✻✻✻✻✻✻✻✻✻

Regular Cast

MRS. SLOCOMBE	Mollie Sugden
MR. HUMPHRIES	John Inman
MR. LUCAS	Trevor Bannister
CAPTAIN PEACOCK	Frank Thornton
MR. GOLDBERG	Alfie Bass
MISS BRAHMS	Wendy Richard
MR. RUMBOLD	Nicholas Smith
YOUNG MR. GRACE	Harold Bennett
MR. HARMON	Arthur English
MISS BAKEWELL	Penny Irving
NURSE	Vivienne Johnson

✻✻✻✻✻✻✻✻✻✻✻✻✻✻✻✻✻✻✻✻✻✻

Episode Ratings

★★★★ *Super*

★★★ *Jolly good*

★★ *Nothing special*

★ *Not up to scratch*

The Junior
★★★★

First transmitted: October 19, 1979 BBC1, UK

MR. WEBSTER	*Tony Sympson*
MR. BAKEWELL	*Jeffrey Gardner*
IVY	*Hilda Fenemore*
CUSTOMERS	*Harold Berens, Morris Barry,*
	Bernard Stone
WARWICK	*Jimmy Mac*

A vacancy appears in Grace Brothers' menswear department, so management decides to advertise for a junior. But the only applicant is Mr. Goldberg, who threatens Captain Peacock's position with his memories of their army days.

☞ *Morris Barry directed three black-and-white Doctor Who stories, including "The Tomb of the Cybermen."*

Strong Stuff This Insurance
★★★★

First transmitted: October 26, 1979 BBC1, UK

Directed by Gordon Elsbury; dance arranged by Sheila O'Neill

BALLET MISTRESS	*Amanda Barrie*
STAFF NURSE	*Joy Allen*
DOCTOR	*Imogen Bickford Smith*
THE DRESSING GOWN	*Geraldine Gardner*
SECOND CUSTOMER	*Jennifer Guy*

Grace Brothers arranges a group insurance scheme for the staff, but to take part on the best terms, they all have to make themselves as fit as possible before their medical examinations.

☞ *Amanda Barrie plays Alma Baldwin in Coronation Street, Britain's most popular series.*

The Apartment
★★★

First transmitted: November 2, 1979 BBC1, UK

Directed by Gordon Elsbury and David Croft

THE BLAZER	*Jeffrey Holland*

Mrs. Slocombe is moving to a new home, but while her furniture is in transit, the new flat is occupied by squatters. So Young Mr. Grace lets her move into a vacant apartment in the store's Furniture Fittings Department and set up house. Things work fine until transport troubles lead Mr. Humphries to move in with her.

☞ *Repeat Business: Jeffrey Holland wanted the Afro Pants in "The Old Order Changes."*

sporran
in traditional Scottish dress, a small pouch or purse that is hung from the front of one's belt

Mrs. Slocombe, Senior Person
★★★

First transmitted: November 9, 1979 BBC1, UK

MISS COMLOZI	*Avril Angers*
THE PLASTIC MAC	*Gorden Kaye*
FIRST CUSTOMER	*Derrie Powell*

Mrs. Slocombe applies for promotion, and when Mr. Rumbold falls ill, she is given his job. But despite Mr. Humphries' support, she finds her new position uncomfortable.

☞ *Hasn't This Happened Before? Well, there was the time that Mr. Grainger took over for Mr. Rumbold.*

☞ *Gorden Kaye contributed the idea for much of the character of the "flash" photographer who manages to nonplus even Mr. Humphries. Kaye suggested that the photographer be a Scotsman who hid his camera in his* sporran *and ad-libbed the reference to Candid Cameron. This led David Croft to allow him to write his own spiel as the reporter who introduced each episode of Come Back, Mrs. Noah.*

The Hero
★★★

First transmitted: November 16, 1979 BBC1, UK
Directed by Gordon Elsbury

MR. FRANCO	*Jackie "Mr. TV" Pallo*
THE SHRUNKEN SOCK	*Raymond Bowers*

Captain Peacock develops a boil in an embarrassing spot, but he's more embarrassed when a member of another department broadcasts the news round the store. He challenges him to a boxing match but falls prey to his natural cowardice as the moment of truth approaches. Only Mr. Humphries can save his honor.

☞ *Jackie Pallo was a wrestler turned actor whose father had been a boxer!*

Anything You Can Do
★★★

First transmitted: November 23, 1979 BBC1, UK
Directed by Gordon Elsbury

CANTEEN MANAGERESS	*Doremy Vernon*
SIGNOR BALLI	*Ronnie Brody*
WARWICK	*Jimmy Mac*
MOHAMMAD	*Mohammad Shamsi*
LIFT GIRLS	*Sue Bishop, Belinda Lee*

The canteen food is going from bad to worse. When the staff complain, the manageress calls her staff out on strike. So the Ladies' and Gents' departments decide to staff the canteen themselves.

☞ *Promotion: Doremy Vernon finally becomes the Canteen Manageress and remains in that post until the series ends.*

☞ *Warwick had previously appeared in "The Junior"; Ronnie Brody would return in "The Night Club."*

The Agent
★★

First transmitted: November 30, 1979 BBC1, UK
Directed by Gordon Elsbury

MR. PATEL	*Renu Setna*
THE LOUD SWEATER	*Jeffrey Segal*
MRS. MAXWELL	*Peggy Ann Clifford*
AMANDA	*Marella Oppenheim*

To supplement his salary, Mr. Goldberg sets up an employment agency and tries to find positions to suit the more talented members of the staff.

The Punch and Judy Affair
★★★★

First transmitted: December 26, 1979 BBC1, UK

CANTEEN MANAGERESS	*Doremy Vernon*
IVY	*Hilda Fenemore*

In the aftermath of a strike in which the characters of the cast did not participate, relations between the strikers and the non-strikers remain bitter. To try and regain favor, the staff of Grace Brothers' Ladies' and Gentlemen's departments stage a life-size Punch and Judy show to entertain the children of the staff. This explains why Mrs. Slocombe intervenes when Mr. Lucas starts to slap Miss Brahms around, and why Captain Peacock has to go to the Devil, as things run out of control, despite Mr. Humphries' efforts as director.

Eighth
SEASON

first broadcast on BBC1 in

19**81**

By Jeremy Lloyd and David Croft
Produced by David Croft; directed by John Kilby

Regular Cast

MRS. SLOCOMBE ....Mollie Sugden
MR. HUMPHRIES ....John Inman
CAPTAIN PEACOCK ....Frank Thornton
MISS BRAHMS ....Wendy Richard
MR. RUMBOLD ....Nicholas Smith
MR. SPOONER.....................Mike Berry
OLD MR. GRACE ....Kenneth Waller
MR. HARMON ....Arthur English
NURSE ....Vivienne Johnson

☞ *The year's break between seasons doesn't indicate any-thing sinister; established BBC series take a break to give the writers a chance to recharge or work on new ideas.*

Episode Ratings

★ ★ ★ ★ *Super*
★ ★ ★ *Jolly good*
★ ★ *Nothing special*
★ *Not up to scratch*

Is It Catching?
★ ★ ★

First transmitted: April 9, 1981 BBC1, UK
MR. GROSSMAN ....*Milo Sperber*
YOUNG MR. GRACE ....*Harold Bennett*
CANTEEN MANAGERESS ....*Doremy Vernon*
DOCTOR ....*John D. Collins*

Has Mr. Humphries been mixing with the Marines? Well, no, but he *has* contracted Marines' Disease, and the whole depart-ment is placed in isolation as a result.

☞ *Goodbye to Young Mr. Grace, who never appears again after this episode, though he contin-ues to be mentioned. Harold Bennett, who was 82 years old, had hoped to return after a rest, but it was not to be.*

A Personal Problem
★ ★

First transmitted: April 16, 1981 BBC1, UK
MR. GROSSMAN ....*Milo Sperber*
SECRETARY ....*Debbie Linden*
MRS. PEACOCK ....*Diana King*
TRAMP ....*Jack Haig*

Captain Peacock is having trouble both at work and with his marriage, and the two come together once he comes to believe that his wife is having an affair with Mr. Rumbold.

☞ *New secretary Debbie Linden was, like her pre-decessor Penny Irving, an ex-Page Three Girl.*

☞ *Hasn't This Happened Before? Well, yes, there was that time two years ago when Mrs. Peacock thought her husband was having an affair with Mr. Rumbold's secretary.*

☞ *The late Jack Haig played Leclerc in 'Allo, 'Allo.*

Front Page Story
★ ★ ★

First transmitted: April 23, 1981 BBC1, UK

MR. GROSSMAN	...............*Milo Sperber*
SECRETARY	..................*Debbie Linden*
MAN WITH MUSTACHE	
..................*Michael Sharvell-Martin*	
MISS HURST	...................*Jennifer Guy*
MISS HEPBURN	.............*Dawn Perllman*
MISS COLEMAN	................*Denise Distel*

Old Mr. Grace decrees that Grace Brothers should have a new in-store magazine, and he appoints Mr. Humphries as its editor. Mr. Humphries' main interest is gossip, while Old Mr. Grace can't wait to see the centerfold.

Sit Out
★ ★ ★

First transmitted: April 30, 1981 BBC1, UK

MR. GROSSMAN	...............*Milo Sperber*
SECRETARY	..................*Debbie Linden*
VIRGINIA EDWARDS	..........*Louise Burton*

Business in the Ladies' and Gents' Ready-to-Wear departments is so poor that the staff are asked to take a 10-percent cut in their wages. They rebel and stage a rooftop protest.

Heir Apparent
★ ★ ★

First transmitted: May 7, 1981 BBC1, UK

MR. GROSSMAN	...............*Milo Sperber*
SECRETARY	..................*Debbie Linden*

When Old Mr. Grace sees an early photograph of Mr. Humphries' mother, he's amazed to recognize a face from his past. Mr. Humphries' graceful movement has long been noted, but now it seems that he may be a Grace himself.

Closed Circuit
★ ★

First transmitted: May 14, 1981 BBC1, UK

MR. KLEIN	.......................*Benny Lee*
SECRETARY	..................*Debbie Linden*
MR. FORTESCUE	...............*Gorden Kaye*
HEADMASTER	............*Nicholas McArdle*
SECOND WAITER	............*John D. Collins*

Grace Brothers decide to show advertisements on closed-circuit television, and Miss Brahms attracts attention.

☞ *Repeat Business? That waiter must've just got struck off, as John D. Collins played a doctor five weeks ago.*

(to) get struck off
to have one's license removed, especially with regard to a physician whose name has been taken off the medical registry

The Erotic Dreams of Mrs. Slocombe ★ ★

First transmitted: May 21, 1981 BBC1, UK

MR. KLEIN	.......................*Benny Lee*
SECRETARY	.................*Debbie Linden*
OLD MAN	........................*Jack Haig*
LADY CUSTOMER	..........*Brenda Cowling*

Mrs. Slocombe dreams of a romantic involvement with Mr. Humphries. That's alright—but when she decides to turn her dreams into reality, the senior salesman makes every attempt to ensure he *isn't* free, as she turns to the bottle.

☞ *Repeat Business: Jack Haig has cleaned himself up since he played a tramp five weeks ago.*

Roots?
★ ★

First transmitted: December 24, 1981 BBC1, UK

MR. KLEIN	.......................*Benny Lee*
SECRETARY	..................*Louise Burton*

Old Mr. Grace is celebrating his ninetieth birthday. While the other departments are already buying gifts, the first floor staff can't decide on an appropriate gift, but they eventually decide to buy him a coat of arms. They find it difficult to trace his roots, however, and they end up rehearsing Welsh, Scottish, and Yokel tributes before reaching a surprising conclusion as to the Graces' ancestry, which leads to a revival of the Black and White Minstrel Show.

Ninth
SEASON

first broadcast on BBC1 in

19**83**

By Jeremy Lloyd and David Croft
Produced and directed by Bob Spiers;
executive producer, David Croft

Regular Cast

MR. HUMPHRIES	*John Inman*
MRS. SLOCOMBE	*Mollie Sugden*
CAPTAIN PEACOCK	*Frank Thornton*
MISS BRAHMS	*Wendy Richard*
MR. RUMBOLD	*Nicholas Smith*
MR. SPOONER	*Mike Berry*
MR. HARMAN	*Arthur English*
MISS BELFRIDGE	*Candy Davis*

Episode Ratings

★★★★ *Super*
★★★ *Jolly good*
★★ *Nothing special*
★ *Not up to scratch*

Sweet Smell of Success
★★

First transmitted: April 22, 1983 BBC1, UK

CANTEEN MANAGERESS	*Doremy Vernon*
MRS. PEACOCK	*Diana King*
HANDSOME CUSTOMER	*Michael Sharvell Martin*
MILITARY CUSTOMER	*Rex Robinson*

Mrs. Slocombe develops a perfume that attracts the opposite sex and suggests that the staff sell it on the side to boost their earnings. Captain Peacock is dubious until he encounters its effects himself, but then he finds that most of all, it attracts trouble.

Conduct Unbecoming
★★★

First transmitted: April 29, 1983 BBC1, UK

TIGHTS CUSTOMER	*Frances Bennett*
WOMAN	*Gilda Perry*
MR. WAGSTAFF	*Tony Sympson*

When Mr. Humphries argues with his mother and is forced to leave home at last, he's hardly his usual gay self. Then money turns up missing from the till, and the evidence points his way.

☞ *Tony Sympson had previously played Grace Brothers' Mr. Webster and a customer.*

Memories Are Made of This

★★

First transmitted: May 6, 1983 BBC1, UK

CANTEEN MANAGERESS	....*Doremy Vernon*
MR. WALPOLE	...................*Jess Conrad*
FISHERMAN	...............*Ballard Berkeley*

Mr. Walpole, the store's golf pro, tries to improve Captain Peacock's golf. But when his swing catches Mrs. Slocombe on the forehead, she becomes a little girl once more.

☞ *Ballard Berkeley played the Major in Fawlty Towers.*

Calling All Customers

★★★

First transmitted: May 13, 1983 BBC1, UK

TRUCK DRIVERS	...*Nosher Powell, Ron Tarr*
CB VOICES	..*Vicki Michelle, Robbie Coltrane*

Grace Brothers decides to advertise on Citizens' Band radio, and the staff find themselves performing a play. But when Mrs. Slocombe gives out her details, she causes chaos on the roads and attracts the sort of customer the store could do without.

☞ *Vicki Michelle had made the pilot episode of 'Allo, 'Allo shortly before this episode.*

☞ *Robbie Coltrane now plays Fitz in the top-rated psychological thriller series, Cracker.*

pay rise
pay raise

Monkey Business

★★★★

First transmitted: May 20, 1983 BBC1, UK

MR. KAGATO	.................*Eifa Kusuhara*
SECRETARY AT NUMBER TEN	*John D. Collins*
FUR COAT CUSTOMER	.......*John Biggersby*
HIS SECRETARY	...............*Lisa Anselmi*
MR. YAMOTO	...............*Kristopher Kum*
MONKEY	.......................*Rusty Goffe*
VOICE OF MRS. THATCHER	......*Jan Ravens*

The staff of Grace Brothers are horrified when their **pay rise** is canceled and fear that a Japanese takeover may be imminent. They take their protests to Number Ten Downing Street, where Mrs. Slocombe speaks to President Reagan on the hot line and gives him a piece of her mind, and Mr. Humphries turns out to be Mrs. Thatcher's blue-eyed boy. But an escaped monkey proves to have more control over the situation than the prime minister.

☞ *A general election was called after this episode was produced, and the BBC considered dropping the episode for fear it might influence the result!*

☞ *Hasn't This Happened Before? Well, there was that takeover attempt in (curiously enough) "Takeover."*

Lost and Found

★★★

First transmitted: May 27, 1983 BBC1, UK

CANTEEN MANAGERESS	.....*Doremy Vernon*
MR. WINSTON	...................*Peter Cleall*
CUSTOMER	...............*Norman Mitchell*

Mrs. Slocombe loses her pussy, and it seems that only Mr. Humphries can take its place.

☞ *This episode was originally to have been shown before "Monkey Business."*

Tenth

SEASON

first broadcast on BBC1 in

19 85

By Jeremy Lloyd and David Croft;
scripts by Jeremy Lloyd
Produced and directed by Martin Shardlow;
executive producer, David Croft

✳✳✳✳✳✳✳✳✳✳✳✳✳✳✳✳✳✳✳✳✳

Regular Cast

MR. HUMPHRIES	John Inman
MRS. SLOCOMBE	Mollie Sugden
CAPTAIN PEACOCK	Frank Thornton
MISS BRAHMS	Wendy Richard
MR. RUMBOLD	Nicholas Smith
MR. SPOONER	Mike Berry
MR. HARMAN	Arthur English
MISS BELFRIDGE	Candy Davis

✳✳✳✳✳✳✳✳✳✳✳✳✳✳✳✳✳✳✳✳✳

Episode Ratings

★ ★ ★ ★ *Super*
★ ★ ★ *Jolly good*
★ ★ *Nothing special*
★ *Not up to scratch*

Goodbye Mrs. Slocombe
★ ★ ★ ★

First transmitted: February 18, 1985 BBC1, UK

CANTEEN MANAGERESS .....*Doremy Vernon*
MISS FEATHERSTONE ......*Joanna Dunham*
CUSTOMER ....*Elizabeth Stewart*

Mrs. Slocombe returns from a bout of illness to find that Grace Brothers has instituted an early retirement policy—and she's first for the chop. Her replacement is tactless and undiplomatic, and the staff revolt en masse. But Mrs. Slocombe refuses to leave the store and decides to take any job on offer in order to remain. When the senior staff realize that they could be next, they decide to take radical measures.

☞ *The first episode of Wendy Richard's new venture, the soap opera EastEnders, was transmitted the day after this episode.*

☞ *This episode marked the debut of a revamped title sequence in which the credits rose as if in the lift.*

☞ *The end credits for this episode show Mr. Humphries talking to himself in drag.*

☞ *All this talk of the executive dining room is interesting, as the dining room was merged with the staff canteen back in "Up Captain Peacock" in accordance with work and factory regulations.*

Grounds for Divorce
★ ★

First transmitted: February 25, 1985 BBC1, UK

MISS BAGNOLD ....*Maggie Henderson*
MRS. PEACOCK ....*Diana Lambert*
CUSTOMER ....*Philip Kendal*

When the staff of Grace Brothers discover Captain Peacock has a shameful secret, they decide to help in every way they can. But while the answer to the Captain's problems lies in his own hands, his attempts to discourage his unwanted admirer take Mr. Humphries' breath away.

☞ *Face-Lift! Mrs. Peacock used to be played by Diana King—now she's Diana Lambert.*

The Hold-Up
★

First transmitted: March 4, 1985 BBC1, UK

BURGLARS *Michael Attwell, Paul Humpoletz*
POLICEMAN ....*Ian Collier*

When the staff stay overnight to **stock-take**, they find they are not alone. Mr. Rumbold and Miss Belfridge might have slipped off to the back row of the cinema, but there are two uninvited guests in the building. Captain Peacock suggests that they might earn a rise if they capture the burglars themselves, but he and Mr. Spooner get themselves captured. Enter the Gumby clan (alias Mr. Harman and Mrs. Slocombe) and Italian Tony (alias Mr. Humphries), and it's not long before things go to pieces.

☞ *Michael Attwell played Wendy Richard's brother Kenny Beale in EastEnders.*

☞ *This episode was written to give Arthur English the opportunity to reprise the Spiv character from his stage shows.*

(to) stock-take
to take inventory of
merchandise

Gambling Fever

★★

First transmitted: March 11, 1985 BBC1, UK

CANTEEN MANAGERESS ....*Doremy Vernon*
CUSTOMER ....*Harriet Reynolds*
SEYMOUR ....*Keith Hodiak*

Grace Brothers has installed closed-circuit television as a security measure, but the staff find a way to exploit it which couldn't be more insecure.

☞ *Hasn't This Happened Before? Yes—they installed closed-circuit television back in "Big Brother."*

The Night Club

★★★★

First transmitted: March 18, 1985 BBC1, UK

CANTEEN MANAGERESS ....*Doremy Vernon*
SEYMOUR ....*Keith Hodiak*
MEN IN CINEMA *Ronnie Brody, Ray Gatenby*

Mr. Grace decides the store could make money in the evenings after shopping hours and expects the staff to come up with ideas. Their idea is a good one, but their advertising campaign leaves a lot to be desired. The audience for a sex film is hardly the clientele the store wants to attract.

☞ *The end credits for this episode are shown projected onto the cinema screen.*

☞ *Hasn't This Happened Before? Yes, the staff made an advert both in "It Pays to Advertise" and "Calling All Customers."*

Friends and Neighbours

★★

First transmitted: March 25, 1985 BBC1, UK

CANTEEN MANAGERESS ....*Doremy Vernon*
MRS. PEACOCK ....*Diana Lambert*
MRS. RUMBOLD ....*Jean Challis*
LADY CUSTOMER ....*Carol Cleveland*
CEDRIC ....*Felipe Izquierdo*

The staff are offered accommodation on the premises to save them time and traveling expenses. But they soon discover that flat sharing isn't a bed of roses, and that whatever else they might save, they're guaranteed to lose their tempers.

☞ *Carol Cleveland was Monty Python's regular female cast member.*

The Pop Star

★★★

First transmitted: April 1, 1985 BBC1, UK
Choreographed by Chris Power

CANTEEN MANAGERESS ....*Doremy Vernon*
TV PRESENTER ....*Nick Ross*
SEYMOUR ....*Keith Hodiak*
TV DIRECTOR ....*Charles Nicklin*
SAM, THE DIRECTOR'S ASSISTANT
..............................*Suzy Aitchison*
CLEANERS ......*Mary Bradley, Joan Dainty*

Life's full of ups and downs for Mr. Spooner when he's sent to the lifts as a punishment for being late. Though he was ostracized in the canteen, his performance at the staff concert is noted by the local paper, and the road to fame beckons. The rest of the staff feel they should share in his good fortune and insist on backing him when he makes his TV debut.

☞ *Nick Ross, a BBC current affairs presenter, plays himself.*

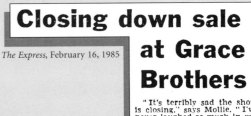

The Express, February 16, 1985

Closing down sale at Grace Brothers

"It's terribly sad the show is closing," says Mollie. "I've never laughed so much in my life as I have at Grace Brothers.

"I know Mrs Slocombe is fearsome. But I've grown very fond of the old thing. She's so vulnerable underneath all that flounce. But between you and me, she may not disappear at all!"

The cast's big secret ploy to save their jobs is a whole new series.

"This show is closing," says Mollie. "But it looks like ~~we'll be s~~ ving ~~nother~~
~~ng t~~ e ~~rs~~

Are You Being Served? aired for the first time in the United States during the summer of 1987, on 24 PBS stations. It has remained on the air in one region or another of this country ever since. The broadcast audience has grown significantly over the years, and the show can now be seen from sea to shining sea—even in Alaska. American audiences have become more fond of the program and its cast of characters over time. The demographic range of the audience for *Are You Being Served?* is as broad as its geographic range. The show is popular with conservative Southerners and politically correct San Franciscans, men and women, young and old, straights and gays. PBS stations report that individual members pledge money specifically to keep the show on the air.

Of all those who have taken *Are You Being Served?* to their hearts and television screens, perhaps none is as avid a fan as Marcia Richards, who, in 1992, formed the *Are You Being Served?* International Fan Club. A bubbly, outgoing businesswoman and homemaker, Richards was living in Memphis, Tennessee, when local PBS station WKNO began airing the program. After learning that there was no fan club for the show's many admirers, Richards set about forming one. Now based near Dallas, Texas, she boasts of 900 club members in this country, Britain, and Australia.

Fan club members, according to Richards, include people from all walks of life. "I've got doctors, lawyers, lots of retirees—in fact, two people in the club are 100 years old—and some teenagers who have joined with their parents." Fan club members receive a quarterly newsletter that brings them up to date on the lives of the cast and includes articles, poetry, and cartoons relating to the program.

Richards has her own thoughts as to why the program remains so popular. "Once you start watching the show, the chemistry clicks and you can't help but think of the cast members as part of your family," she says. One fan club member, a psychiatrist, told Richards that watching *Are You Being Served?* is "mentally healthy. When you watch it, you can get away from everyday hassles and worries."

Marcia Richards, AYBS? Fan Club President

"Maybe it's the actors' British accents, but they seem to get away with saying certain things that others couldn't. So in this way the show is something of a guilty pleasure [for its audience]. It's also popular because of the cast's chemistry and easy banter."— David Rubinsohn, Director of Broadcasting at WHYY in Philadelphia

Mollie and fans.

Cast look-alikes.

The fan club is clearly a labor of love for Richards. "I put a lot of myself into the club, and it has given me so much," she explains. "I have met wonderful people who have become close friends." In addition to the fan club members, Richards is also in contact with the cast members of *Are You Being Served?* "They are so overwhelmed by how the show has been received all over the world, and have a lot of gratitude for the attention they are still getting," she says.

Richards struck up a particularly close friendship with *Grace and Favour* (called *Are You Being Served? Again!* in the US) cast member Billy Burden, with whom she corresponded for more than a year and spoke to on the telephone several times a week. She had planned to visit him at his home in England in August 1994, but, sadly, Burden died unexpectedly in June. Richards traveled to the West Country in England for his funeral where, since Burden had never married and had no immediate relatives at the service, Richards was treated as family and asked to stand at the head of the mourners' receiving line. "It was a very mixed experience for me," she says. "I had come to love him with all my heart and was so sad when he died—but there I was, being treated like a queen! In some ways, it was like a fairy tale." The fairy tale extended to Burden's will: Richards was named one of his primary heirs and inherited the extensive television and theater memorabilia he had collected during the decades he spent in show business.

When Marcia Richards first watched *Are You Being Served?*, she told her husband, Tommy, "I don't know what it is, but I feel like I'm going to be directly connected with this." She wanted to know what had happened to the cast members since the program first aired in Great Britain and so turned to a higher power for guidance, saying in her prayers, "I know that you're not really supposed to pray for material things, and I don't worship these people, but I think they're great and I would love to be able somehow, someday to meet them. If you think this is good for me, I know that this will happen." And so it did.

Marcia Richards can be contacted c/o *Are You Being Served?* International Fan Club, P.O. Box 451087, Garland, TX 75045-1087.

JOHN INMAN'S RECIPE FOR
Tuna Surprise

You will need:

1	198g (7oz.) can tuna fish		1	medium sized onion (or leek)
1	198g (7oz.) can sweet corn (with peppers is nice)		4	good handfuls of ribbon pasta
1	can condensed cream of mushroom soup			salt and pepper
1	Tablespoon of dry sherry			3 oz. of grated cheese for the top

Method: Add a pinch of salt and a teaspoon of olive oil to a saucepan of water and bring to a boil. The olive oil will prevent the pasta from sticking. Finely chop the onion (or leek) and add this to the water as soon as you have put the pasta in. Stir well and leave to cook. Drain the tuna then place it with all the remaining ingredients (except the cheese) in a large bowl and stir together.

When the pasta is cooked, drain it and then stir the pasta and onion into the mixture in the bowl. Empty the whole lot into an oven-proof dish and cover with about 3 oz. of grated cheese. Cook at 200°C/400°F for 15 minutes until the cheese is brown and bubbles.

Courtesy of *The AYBS? Fan Club Newsletter*, May 1994

"I like to go to bed with a smile on my face. Why are you taking *Are You Being Served?* off the air? I'll start paying you when you put it back on."— a viewer at KEUD in Salt Lake City, Utah, a station that ranks *Are You Being Served?* among its most highly watched programs

❋

"We are made happier each night by concluding our day with *Are You Being Served?* It has changed our lives."—a fan

Grace and Favour

(KNOWN AS *ARE YOU BEING SERVED? AGAIN!* IN THE US)

WHEN *ARE YOU BEING SERVED?* ENDED IN 1985, THE cast suggested that a spin-off series might follow, as Jeremy Lloyd and David Croft had assured them that while the department store format was exhausted, they could always move the characters on to a new location. Nevertheless, it was seven years before the staff of Grace Brothers returned to the TV screen, with a remarkably topical plot. In contrast to the original series, *Grace and Favour* is a serial, with plots running over from one episode to another, and guest characters reappearing regularly.

In the aftermath of Young Mr. Grace's death, Grace Brothers' department store has finally closed down. The staff of the Ladies' and Gentlemen's Ready-to-Wear departments, the faithful few who stayed right through to the closing-down sale, gather for the reading of his will, only to discover that their pension fund has been used to buy a dilapidated manor house, now a hotel run (to their horror) by Mr. Rumbold.

With a tiny income to rely on, they decide to staff the hotel themselves. They're joined at their new home by Miss Lovelock, the nurse who brought on Young Mr. Grace's fatal heart attack, and the inhabitants of a nearby farm. Mavis Moulterd soon takes a shine to Mr. Humphries, while her odoriferous father proves to be a ghost from Mrs. Slocombe's racy past.

Grace *and* Favour's

First
SEASON

first broadcast on BBC1 in

19**92**

By Jeremy Lloyd and David Croft
Produced and directed by Mike Stephens

✳✳✳✳✳✳✳✳✳✳✳✳✳✳✳✳✳✳✳✳✳

Regular Cast

MR. HUMPHRIES ....*John Inman*
MRS. SLOCOMBE ....*Mollie Sugden*
MISS BRAHMS ....*Wendy Richard*
CAPTAIN PEACOCK ....*Frank Thornton*
MR. RUMBOLD ....*Nicholas Smith*
MAURICE MOULTERD ....*Billy Burden*
MAVIS MOULTERD ....*Fleur Bennett*
MISS JESSICA LOVELOCK ......*Joanne Heywood*

✳✳✳✳✳✳✳✳✳✳✳✳✳✳✳✳✳✳✳✳✳

Episode Ratings

★ ★ ★ ★ *Super*
★ ★ ★ *Jolly good*
★ ★ *Nothing special*
★ *Not up to scratch*

Episode One
★ ★

First transmitted: January 10, 1992 BBC1, UK

MISS PRESCOTT	*Shirley Cheriton*
MR. THORPE	*Michael Bilton*
SECRETARY	*Penny Gonshaw*

Young Mr. Grace passes on at last, while playing in the surf with his nurse and companion Jessica Lovelock. Though his equipment was a bit elderly, it seemed to be in perfect working order, but when her bikini top pops off, so does he. He leaves his fortune to a home for fallen women, and the staff of Grace Brothers find they're left to make a living from the run-down country manor house he bought with the proceeds of their pension scheme. Mr. Rumbold's ever-dependable management techniques have ensured that the hotel needs new staff, and Mr. Humphries is forced to start chasing 𝔟𝔦𝔯𝔡𝔰.

☞ *Grace and Favour began a few months after the death at sea of British press tycoon Robert Maxwell (inspiration for To the Manor Born's Richard De Vere) and the subsequent discovery by his staff that his empire was on the verge of collapse and that he'd bled their pension funds dry.*

☞ *Where Mrs. Peacock has gone is anyone's guess, but Mrs. Rumbold has run off with Mr. Prentice of Tools and Hardware.*

𝔟𝔦𝔯𝔡
a woman

☞ *After having filmed 69 episodes of the first series entirely in the studio, the cast finally gets to go on location.*

☞ *For the first time ever, Mrs. Slocombe's pussy finally appears, emerging from her portable kennel at Millstone Manor.*

☞ *From the moment that the lift door jams, the opening few minutes of this episode give every memorable joke from the original series one last outing.*

☞ *Michael Bilton, veteran actor and co-star of the BBC sitcoms Waiting for God and To the Manor Born, died in November 1993. Here he plays Mr. Grace's solicitor, the junior partner of Thorpe, Thorpe, and Thorpe.*

☞ *Shirley Cheriton was, like Wendy Richard, one of the original cast of the BBC soap opera East-Enders; she played Debbie Wilkins.*

Episode Two
★ ★

First transmitted: January 17, 1992 BBC1, UK

JOSEPH LEE	*Andrew Joseph*
MR. THORPE	*Michael Bilton*
MISS PRESCOTT	*Shirley Cheriton*
FOX HUNTER	*Martyn Townsend*

Activity in the early hours gives the staff of Grace Brothers a sleepless night. So, too, do the established residents of Millstone Manor, whether they be human, animal, or something in between. Mrs. Slocombe gets a shock when she tries to arouse Mr. Humphries, while Mavis shows Mr. Humphries how to light her fire, and Captain Peacock gets Mrs. Slocombe into trouble on the way to the village.

Episode Three
★ ★ ★

First transmitted: January 24, 1992 BBC1, UK

MR. THORPE	*Michael Bilton*
MISS PRESCOTT	*Shirley Cheriton*
USHER	*Roger Winslett*
CLERK	*James Walker*
SIR ROBERT	*Eric Dodson*
CELIA LITTLEWOOD	*Diane Holland*
POLICE INSPECTOR	*Geoffrey Greenhill*
JOSEPH LEE	*Andrew Joseph*
COMMENTATOR	*Chris Barrie*
STUNTS	*Roy Alon, Bill Weston*

Mrs. Slocombe comes to court, charged with speeding in a stolen gypsy cart with her legs in the air. The indecent exposure charge is dropped, but the local paper managed to get a snap of her as she flashed past. Miss Lovelock offers Captain Peacock a lift, but he prefers traveling to court on Moulterd's pig cart. Attorney Thorpe's defense strategy relies on character witnesses—and Mrs. Slocombe certainly knows some characters.

☞ *Diane Holland had played Yvonne Stuart Hargreaves in Jimmy Perry and David Croft's holiday camp series Hi-de-Hi!, and she reappears in season two of Grace and Favour, as does Sir Robert.*

☞ *Chris Barrie plays Rimmer in Red Dwarf and stars in The Brittas Empire, produced by Grace and Favour's Mike Stephens.*

Episode Four
★ ★

First transmitted: January 31, 1992 BBC1, UK

GYPSY	*Andrew Joseph*
CAR DRIVER	*Jeremy Lloyd*
MRS. CLEGHAMPTON	*Maggie Holland*
MR. VOLPONE	*Gordon Peters*
MR. FROBISHER	*Gregory Cox*
STUNTS	*Roy Alon, Bill Weston*

The hotel has a booking at last. But Mr. Rumbold still hasn't recruited any staff, so everyone must muck in if they're to make Millstone Manor presentable before the Americans get there. Then two applicants arrive—but neither seems able to stand on his own two feet.

dicky
shirt collar

a blow
a try, as in "to give someone a blow at something"; a blow at the organ is a pump of the organ's bellows

Episode Five
★ ★ ★

First transmitted: February 7, 1992 BBC1, UK

MR. FROBISHER	*Gregory Cox*
MR. MAXWELL	*Paul Cooper*

With no new recruits, it's unfortunate that a photographer is coming to snap the staff. Mr. Humphries slips into the barman's trousers, Miss Brahms and Mrs. Slocombe get maid up, and Captain Peacock waits in vain for his **dicky** to behave. Then Mrs. Slocombe's pussy goes bump in the night.

Episode Six
★ ★ ★

First transmitted: February 14, 1992 BBC1, UK

MR. FROBISHER	*Gregory Cox*

With Miss Lovelock's recommendations in place, the hotel is at last in business, as a group of elderly Americans visiting the ruins of Europe arrives to see the relics of Grace Brothers. But while the staff do their best to extend hospitality, they're out of their depth when it comes to village traditions, though Mrs. Slocombe agrees to give Mr. Rumbold **a blow** at the organ.

Grace and Favour's

Second SEASON

first broadcast on BBC1 in

19**93**

By Jeremy Lloyd and David Croft
Produced and directed by Mike Stephens

✽✽✽✽✽✽✽✽✽✽✽✽✽✽✽✽✽✽✽✽✽✽✽

Regular Cast

MR. HUMPHRIES ....*John Inman*

MRS. SLOCOMBE ....*Mollie Sugden*

MISS BRAHMS ....*Wendy Richard*

CAPTAIN PEACOCK ....*Frank Thornton*

MR. RUMBOLD ....*Nicholas Smith*

MAURICE MOULTERD ....*Billy Burden*

MAVIS MOULTERD ....*Fleur Bennett*

MISS JESSICA LOVELOCK ......*Joanne Heywood*

✽✽✽✽✽✽✽✽✽✽✽✽✽✽✽✽✽✽✽✽✽✽✽

Episode Ratings

★ ★ ★ ★ *Super*

★ ★ ★ *Jolly good*

★ ★ *Nothing special*

★ *Not up to scratch*

178

Episode One
★ ★ ★ ★

First transmitted: January 4, 1993 BBC1, UK

INSPECTOR ....*Roger Sloman*
SERGEANT ....*Richard Lumsden*
COLIN ....*Steve Edwin*
RIOT POLICEMAN ....*Steve Whyment*

The Americans are gone, though their chewing gum is sticking around. But when Captain Peacock finds a loaded gun in a drawer, Mr. Humphries thinks it advisable to duck, and the local police overreact just a little, as they investigate the nest of terrorists in their midst.

☞ *Roger Sloman came to Grace and Favour fresh from playing Inspector Deffand in the final season of the BBC detective series Bergerac.*

☞ *Mr. Rumbold still has Fly Fishing by J. R. Hartley outstanding on his library ticket. Never heard of it? Hardly surprising, but everyone in Britain knows it—it was invented for a British commercial where an old man (J. R. Hartley himself, as it turns out) is searching for a copy. The commercial proved so popular that the book was later written to cash in on the interest!*

Episode Two
★ ★ ★ ★

First transmitted: January 11, 1993 BBC1, UK

MR. LUBITCH ....*Leonard Lowe*
CELIA LITTLEWOOD ....*Diane Holland*
MR. THORPE ....*Michael Bilton*
MISS PRESCOTT ....*Shirley Cheriton*
JESSIE ....*Joe Hobbs*
MALCOLM HEATHCLIFF ....*Andrew Barclay*
SIR ROBERT ....*Eric Dodson*

Trouble continues as the staff of Millstone Manor find themselves persuaded to join the village cricket match. Mrs. Slocombe, at least, is delighted—she 𝔟𝔬𝔴𝔩𝔢𝔡 against the RAF during the war, and her 𝔟𝔬𝔲𝔫𝔠𝔢𝔯𝔰 were treated with great respect. But Mr. Humphries is not so pleased—Mavis has proposed to him to discourage her old boyfriend, who bowls for the opposite side.

(to) bowl
in the sport of cricket, throwing the ball to a batsman, the equivalent of baseball's pitching

bouncer
in the sport of cricket, a short-pitched ball delivery that goes about head high to the batsman; also, in popular slang, a woman's breasts

Episode Three
★★★

First transmitted: January 18, 1993 BBC1, UK

CECIL SLOCOMBE ....*Donald Morley*

Forty-two years ago, Mr. Slocombe went to the shops for some butter and never returned. Now, to Mrs. Slocombe's embarrassment, he turns up at Millstone Manor, and to escape him she's forced to fulfill Moulterd's wildest dreams by posing as his wife. But as Cecil Slocombe hopes to buy the manor, desperate measures must be taken if he's not to stay for good.

☞ *Donald Morley had previously played a Grace Brothers' customer during the second series and the security consultant in "Big Brother."*

Episode Four
★★★★

First transmitted: January 25, 1993 BBC1, UK

MUSEUM ATTENDANT ....*Roger Avon*
MUSEUM CURATOR ....*Patrick Fyffe*

When Captain Peacock and Miss Lovelock find the petrified remains of a cat behind an attic wall and donate it to the local museum, strange events afflict Millstone Manor. Moulterd explains that such relics bring good luck and should not be removed. To confirm this, a catalogue of disasters proves him right as the cow dries up, Mrs. Slocombe's drawers fly open, and yellow slime pours from the oven. The staff soon realize that to escape the curse, they must recover Mrs. Slocombe's antique pussy.

Episode Five
★★★

First transmitted: February 1, 1993 BBC1, UK

MALCOLM HEATHCLIFF .....*Andrew Barclay*
HENRY HEATHCLIFF ....*Paul Humpoletz*
POLICEMAN ....*Nick Scott*
LANDLORD ....*Colin Edwynn*
SHIRLEY BRAHMS AS THE DOG
.........................*with Martin Friend*

The staff decide to introduce democracy to the running of Millstone Manor, but the trouble this causes pales in the face of a challenge to a local darts match, which leads to a fight with Mavis' ex-boyfriend Malcolm, and a midnight raid to free the Heathcliffs' sheep.

☞ *Yes, the dog's name really is Shirley Brahms, according to the end credits!*

☞ *This was actually shot as the final episode.*

Episode Six
★★

First transmitted: February 8, 1993 BBC1, UK

MALCOLM HEATHCLIFF .....*Andrew Barclay*
MR. THORPE ....*Michael Bilton*
MRS. CLEGHAMPTON ......*Maggie Holland*
MISS LONG WEE ....*Akemi Otani*

In the time since a group of Mongolian businessmen booked to stay at the manor, their currency has collapsed. So the cultural display they were promised must be done on the cheap. Miss Brahms gives them her Porsche, while Miss Lovelock and Mr. Humphries take to the stage as Romeo and Juliet.

The *Movie*

BY THE LATE 1970S, THE BRITISH FILM INDUSTRY
was in decline, sustained only by big-screen versions of television series.
Unfortunately, most of these films were sorry affairs. Assuming that the audience wouldn't come to the cinema unless enticed by more than they could get
from their televisions, the producers insisted on "big" plots that went much
beyond the story line of the series. Hence, Harold gets married in the *Steptoe
and Son* film, *Up Pompeii!* ends with the eruption of Vesuvius, and *Till Death
Us Do Part* traces Alf Garnett's history back to the Second World War. All of
this was unfortunate, as the series, which depended on the claustrophobic relations between their stars, were less effective when opened out.

The *Are You Being Served?* film follows this pattern closely, as the staff take a
package holiday together while the store is closed for redecoration, but compared to other films based on TV series, this one is rather more successful. The
first half of the film is an expanded TV episode, in which the staff copes with
their variety of customers and indulges in their usual maneuverings while
preparing to leave. Once they reach Spain, their libidos take over as Mr. Lucas
plots to win Miss Brahms, Mrs. Slocombe encourages advances from Captain
Peacock, and Mr. Humphries demonstrates once again his innate style as
things build toward an explosive climax.

Starring

JOHN INMAN
as Mr. Humphries

MOLLIE SUGDEN
as Mrs. Slocombe

FRANK THORNTON
as Captain Peacock

TREVOR BANNISTER
as Mr. Lucas

WENDY RICHARD
as Miss Brahms

ARTHUR BROUGH
as Mr. Grainger

NICHOLAS SMITH
as Mr. Rumbold

HAROLD BENNETT
as Young Mr. Grace

ARTHUR ENGLISH
as Mr. Harman

KARAN DAVID
as Conchita

GLYN HOUSTON
as Cesar Rodriguez

ANDREW SACHS
as Don Carlos Bernardo

NADIM SAWALHA
as the Hat Customer

**JOHN G. HELLER AND
HUGO DE VERNIER**
as the Germans

MONICA GREY
as the Staff Nurse

JENNIFER GRENVILLE
as the Air Hostess

DEREK GRIFFITHS
as the Arab

NADIM SAWALHA
as his Interpreter

PENNY IRVING
as Miss Nicholson

ANDREW MANN
as the Pilot

**MARIANNE BROOME,
NICKI HOWORTH,
AND RICKI HOWARD**
as the Gorgeous Girls

The Movie

*Written by Jeremy Lloyd and David Croft
Produced by Andrew Mitchell; executive
producers, David Croft and Jeremy Lloyd;
directed by Bob Kellett*

Made at EMI Elstree, 1977

Grace Brothers is to close for redecoration, so its staff will holiday together, courtesy of Young Mr. Grace. Mr. Rumbold will accompany them (though Mrs. Peacock, Mrs. Grainger, and Mrs. Rumbold will not). But first there are preparations to make, and the staff must still get through a normal work day. Mrs. Slocombe delivers her pussy to the Animal Hotel Department, Mr. Lucas arrives late, and Young Mr. Grace visits each department in turn. Mrs. Slocombe leads Captain Peacock on, and Mr. Humphries and Mr. Lucas devise a way to measure an Arab sheik's inside leg without touching his flesh, managing to sell 100 balloons in the process. Mr. Harman demonstrates the inflatable lifesaver bra to Miss Brahms, and Mrs. Slocombe has trouble with her injections and her passport photo.

The staff finally fly to the Costa Plonka, where they try to check in at their hotel. Don Carlos Bernardo has their reservation, but he was only expecting two Grace brothers—and is shocked by Mrs. Slocombe and Miss Brahms, whom he assumes to be a drag act. No rooms are available that night, but he can put them up in the new wing—which will be ready the next day. In the meantime, he offers them the pentyhouses, which the staff gratefully accept—but it turns out that they're actually *tenty-houses*. Mr. Harman, however, has been more lucky—but then, he booked as the Earl of Harman (he used to book as a trade union leader but found he couldn't afford the rooms).

As the staff settle down for a night under canvas and a meal under the stars, Carlos is accosted by his brother, the rebel leader Cesar, who demands shelter until the revolution begins—and company for the night. Carlos refuses to give him the chambermaid Conchita (whom he's keeping for himself), interesting him instead in the charms of the English lady—Mrs. Slocombe.

Over dinner, Mr. Lucas sends a note to Miss Brahms inviting her to his tent—but it's misdirected, and as a result, by the end of the evening Captain Peacock is expecting a visit from Miss Brahms, Mrs. Slocombe thinks she'll be spending the night with the Captain, and Mr. Humphries has agreed to give shelter to Conchita. Things really get out of control when a caterpillar drives Miss Brahms from her tent, and Mr. Humphries finds himself entertaining Cesar (killer of twelve men) disguised as Mrs. Slocombe, complete with her wig and a lifesaver bra.

The following morning the revolution dawns. Government troops descend upon the hotel, attempting to arrest Cesar, and the staff find themselves pinned down under fire, without even Mrs. Slocombe's Union Jack bloomers to wave for help. But all's well in the end, as a tank—driven by Young Mr. Grace—arrives to save them.

☞ *Nadim Sawalha is the father of Absolutely Fabulous star Julia Sawalha.*

☞ *Ricki Howard later played Sylvia in Hi-de-Hi!*

☞ *Penny Irving's character was Mr. Rumbold's secretary, Miss Bakewell, on TV, but becomes Young Mr. Grace's secretary, Miss Nicholson, in the film.*

☞ *Marianne Broome is yet another ex-Page Three Girl.*

ARE YOU BEING SERVED?

The Play

Ran June to October 1976 at Winter Gardens,
Blackpool, with the original cast
Written by Jeremy Lloyd and David Croft
Production supervised by David Croft;
directed by Roger Redfarn

Starring

JOHN INMAN
as Mr. Humphries

MOLLIE SUGDEN
as Mrs. Slocombe

FRANK THORNTON
as Captain Peacock

WENDY RICHARD
as Miss Brahms

NICHOLAS SMITH
as Mr. Rumbold

MICHAEL MUNDELL
as Mr. Lucas

LARRY NOBLE
as Mr. Grainger

STUART SHERWIN
as Mr. Mash and
Don Bernardo

BARBARA ROSENBLATT
as the Lady Customer
and Teresa

PETRA SINIAWSKI
as the Nurse
and Conchita

RAYMOND BOWERS
as the Male Customer
and Cesar

After a normal day's work (and trouble
with the lift), the staff of Grace Brothers
go on a holiday during which a series of
mistaken assignations leads them in and
out of each other's tents.

☞ *Short synopsis, but the play and the film had
the same basic plot, though Young Mr. Grace's role
was omitted and Mr. Mash had less to do than Mr.
Harman.*

☞ *Reviews of the play were few and mixed. The
Blackpool diarist of The Stage (Britain's equivalent of Variety) commented on the booming careers
of Frank Thornton, Mollie Sugden, and, in particular, John Inman, and declared it the funniest show
he'd seen in 30 years of summer seasons. In contrast, The Times' political correspondent, Michael
Leapman, who attended the show during the
Labour Party Conference held that year in Blackpool, was relentlessly negative. He declared the play
plotless and worthwhile only for the final line,
which inspired him to launch a competition seeking
appropriate closing lines for other awful shows. As
he admitted he'd never seen the TV series, The
Stage's verdict is perhaps more reliable.*

diarist
columnist

Earlier Books

Are You Being Served?

By Jeremy Lloyd, from the scripts by
Jeremy Lloyd and David Croft
Mayflower Books (a subsidiary of Granada),
1976, £.5 paperback

This book is a collection of short stories
taken from seven episodes.

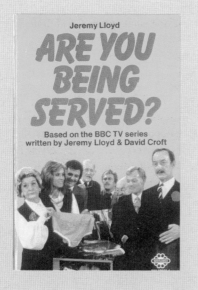

Are You Being Served Abroad?

By Jeremy Lloyd and David Croft
White Lion Books, 1978, £3.25 hardback

This is a novelization of the film.

☞ Both books are out of print.

BEANES OF Boston

Adapted by Jeremy Lloyd, David Croft, Bill
Idelson, and Sheldon Bull
Executive producer Gary Marshall

Starring: **ALAN SUES** as Mr. Humphries
JOHN HILLERMAN as Mr. Peacock
CHARLOTTE RAE as Mrs. Slocombe, and
LORNA PATTERSON as Miss Brahms

Beanes of Boston, the pilot for an American version of *Are You Being Served?*, was made in 1979 by Gary Marshall, then riding high in the Neilson ratings with *Happy Days*, which he had produced and directed, and its spin-offs. At the time, Americanized versions of British series were also doing well, including *Three's Company* (*Man About the House*), *All in the Family* (*Till Death Do Us Part*), and *Sanford and Son* (*Steptoe and Son*). Unfortunately, the *Beanes of Boston* pilot didn't sell.

Jeremy Lloyd's *Laugh-In* partner Alan Sues was cast as Mr. Humphries and played him rather like Paul Lynde, *Bewitched*'s Uncle Arthur. Lloyd later commented that he'd forgotten quite what Sues was like and that he proved to be miscast. John Hillerman, later to become Magnum PI's nemesis Jonathan Quayle Higgins, played Mr. Peacock.

When John Hillerman failed to show
up for a read-through, Jeremy Lloyd
read through his part so well
that Gary Marshall said, "Forget
him, Lloyd's got the part."
But David Croft said Lloyd couldn't
do it as he had more shows to write.
So Lloyd was offered a part in
Happy Days instead, which wasn't to
shoot for 16 weeks, so he couldn't do it.

Among the actors rejected for the
pilot show was the then comparatively
unknown Robin Williams.
"We thought he was terribly good,"
says Jeremy Lloyd, "but couldn't think
what to do with him."

The Australian Version

AUSTRALIA HAD BEEN BUYING BRITISH comedy series ever since its television service started. Initially, the cast or crew of British series were hired to produce further episodes in which some of the cast went "down under" after the original ended, but by the 1970s, it had become quite common for the Australians to produce episodes of their own. In the case of this series, the Australian version began while the original was still on the air.

In 1980 and 1981, John Inman visited Australia to make two series of *Are You Being Served?* Jeremy Lloyd adapted the scripts from his British originals (an experience he claims not to have enjoyed), basing the first season on the seventh season episodes recently shown in Great Britain (and as yet unscreened in Australia), and the second on a selection of older scripts.

Mr. Humphries aside, the characters are renamed versions of the originals, who work in Bone Brothers' department store. Captain Peacock becomes Captain Wagstaff, Mrs. Slocombe is Mrs. Crawford, and Mr. Goldberg is Mr. Mankowitz, while Mr. Rumbold becomes Mr. Dunkling (in the first season) and Mr. Fenwick (in the second). Otherwise, the scripts are little changed, though topical references are deleted in episodes such as "The Apartment."

The Australian Version's

First
SEASON

first broadcast on Channel 10, Australia

19**80**

Adapted by Jeremy Lloyd and Jim Burnett from the original scripts by David Croft and Jeremy Lloyd
Directed by Bob Spiers

Regular Cast

MR. HUMPHRIES ....*John Inman*
MRS. CRAWFORD ....*June Bronhill*
CAPTAIN WAGSTAFF ....*Shane Bourne*
Judith Woodriffe, Anthony Bazell, Peter Collingwood, Basil Clarke, Ken Fraser, and Christine Amor

Keep Fit Down Under

First transmitted: June 16, 1980
(Channel 10, Australia)

Old Mr. Grace lends Mr. Humphries to his Australian cousin, Mr. Bone, who owns a department store where the staff closely resemble the staff of Grace Brothers.

Based in part on "Strong Stuff This Insurance," episode two of season seven.

The Hero

First transmitted: June 23, 1980
(Channel 10, Australia)

Captain Wagstaff is irritated by gossip about an embarrassing ailment and challenges the culprit to a boxing match.

Based on episode five of season seven.

Mrs. Crawford, Senior Person

First transmitted: June 30, 1980
(Channel 10, Australia)

When Mr. Dunkling suffers food poisoning, the staff compete to take his place.

Based on "Mrs. Slocombe, Senior Person," episode four of season seven.

The Agent

First transmitted: July 7, 1980
(Channel 10, Australia)

Mr. Mankowitz moonlights as an employment agent.

Based on episode seven of season seven.

The Apartment

First transmitted: July 14, 1980
(Channel 10, Australia)

Mrs. Crawford moves into the store after a fire but finds her colleagues joining her.

Based on episode three of season seven.

The Junior

First transmitted: July 21, 1980
(Channel 10, Australia)

Mr. Mankowitz takes over, while Mr. Dunkling takes his long service leave.

Loosely based on episode one of season seven.

Punch and Judy

First transmitted: July 28, 1980
(Channel 10, Australia)

A cleaners and caterers' strike hits Bone Brothers.

Based on "The Punch and Judy Affair," the 1979 Christmas special.

Anything You Can Do

First transmitted: August 4, 1980
(Channel 10, Australia)

The third floor takes over when the canteen staff walk out in protest over complaints.

Based on episode six of season seven.

☞ *John Inman and the rest of the Australian cast starred in an hour-long variety special, The John Inman Show, on August 11, 1980.*

The Australian Version's

Second
SEASON

first broadcast on Channel 10, Australia

19**81**

*Adapted by Jeremy Lloyd and Jim Burnett
from the original scripts by David Croft
and Jeremy Lloyd
Directed by Bob Spiers*

✴✴✴✴✴✴✴✴✴✴✴✴✴✴✴✴✴✴✴✴

Regular Cast

MR. HUMPHRIES . . . . *John Inman*
MRS. CRAWFORD . . . . *June Bronhill*
CAPTAIN WAGSTAFF . . . . *Shane Bourne*
*Judith Woodriffe, Anthony Bazell,
Peter Collingwood, Basil Clarke, Ken Fraser,
and Christine Amor*

✴✴✴✴✴✴✴✴✴✴✴✴✴✴✴✴✴✴✴✴

Heir Apparent

First transmitted: February 28, 1981
(Channel 10, Australia)

The staff believe Mr. Humphries might be Mr. Bone's long-lost son.

Based on episode five of season eight.

Camping In

First transmitted: March 7, 1981
(Channel 10, Australia)

The staff stay over in the camping department when a transport strike hits.

Based on episode four of season one.

Front Page Story

First transmitted: March 14, 1981
(Channel 10, Australia)

Mr. Humphries becomes editor of the store magazine.

Based on episode three of season eight.

Our Figures Are Slipping

First transmitted: March 21, 1981
(Channel 10, Australia)

Sales are down, so Mr. Fenwick adopts military sales techniques.

Based on episode three of season one.

Undesirable Alien

First transmitted: March 28, 1981
(Channel 10, Australia)

When Mr. Humphries' visa is declared void, he considers marrying so he can stay in Australia.

Diamonds Are a Man's Best Friend

First transmitted: April 2, 1981
(Channel 10, Australia)

A reward is offered for the recovery of a missing gem.

Based on episode six of season one.

His and Hers

First transmitted: April 9, 1981
(Channel 10, Australia)

A new assistant on the perfume counter begins to attract attention.

Based on episode five of season one.

The Best
of
Are You Being Served?

Written by Don Harris; executive producer John Wilson; producer Laurie Fagen; director Don Hopfer; makeup/wardrobe Kim Pieper; set director Susan Volk

Starring
JOHN INMAN *as Mrs. Humphries*

Mr. Humphries' mother wins a trip to California at her local **chemist.** On the West Coast, she meets a publisher and a number of film, television, and stage producers, all of whom are fascinated by her tales of her son's exciting life at Grace Brothers and express interest in the rights. As she describes these meetings to her son over the phone, he remembers the incidents in question.

☞ *Shot over two days in March 1992 at a Phoenix resort hotel and screened during a PBS pledge drive later that year, these programs presented a series of clips from the original series within a framing plot in which John Inman plays Mr. Humphries' mother, the motorcycle-riding ex-showgirl and usherette so often mentioned but never seen during the series.*

chemist
pharmacy (also a pharmacist)

ARE YOU BEING SERVED, SIR?

The Record

Produced by DTM Records in 1975, this 45 record featured John Inman singing *Are You Being Served, Sir?* on the A side. Backed by *The Teddy Bears' Picnic,* also sung by Inman, it peaked at 39 on the charts.

Delivery Van

In the early 1990s, *Radio Times* offered a set of die-cast vehicles of yesteryear carrying markings derived from classic sitcoms. In addition to the Jones Butchers' and Hodges Greengrocers' vans as seen in *Dad's Army,* the set included the Grace Brothers' delivery van, as *not* seen in *Are You Being Served?*

CHAPTER

5

GRACE
BROS.

Trivia

QUIZ

1

WHERE DOES MR. HUMPHRIES KEEP HIS *slippers?*

a. Under his bed
b. In the oven
c. In his wardrobe

2

WHAT OTHER SIGNIFICANT EVENT TOOK PLACE ON THE DAY STANLEY BALDWIN WAS REPLACED AS *Prime Minister* BY NEVILLE CHAMBERLAIN?

3

WHAT IS THE *largest* SIZE JACKET STOCKED BY GRACE BROTHERS?

a. 40"   b. 44"   c. 48"   d. 52"

4

WHY DOES MR. HUMPHRIES HAVE TO BE HOME BY *1 a.m.?*

5

WHAT DOES MR. RUMBOLD KEEP IN HIS *safe?*

a. Money
b. Racy photos
c. His tea cup and biscuits

See page 205 for the answers.

6

WHEN THE STAFF VOTE TO SACK *Mr. Spooner:*

a. Mr. Humphries and Miss Brahms vote against him.
❑ *True*   *False* ❑
b. Captain Peacock, Mrs. Slocombe, and Mr. Rumbold vote for him.
❑ *True*   *False* ❑

7

IN WHAT YEAR WAS *Millstone Manor* BUILT?

8

Who GAVE MRS. SLOCOMBE THE JOB OF SENIOR SALESWOMAN?

a. Captain Peacock
b. Mr. Rumbold
c. Young Mr. Grace

9

WHAT IS THE NAME OF MRS. SLOCOMBE'S *pussy?*

10

WHY WAS MR. HUMPHRIES FOUND ON THE *doorstep* AS A BABY?

11

MR. *Slocombe* WAS:

a. A vet c. A 𝔭𝔲𝔟𝔩𝔦𝔠𝔞𝔫
b. Retired d. Unemployed

12

MR. RUMBOLD HAS THE FOLLOWING *books* OUTSTANDING ON HIS LIBRARY TICKET:

a. Lolita
b. Fly Fishing by J. R. Hartley
c. Fanny Hill

13

HOW MANY YEARS DID MR. GRAINGER WORK AT GRACE BROTHERS BEFORE HE GOT TO SEE THE *board room?*

a. 17 years c. 37 years
b. 27 years d. 47 years

14

MR. GRAINGER SUGGESTS GIVING MRS. SLOCOMBE A *cyanide tablet* FOR HER BIRTHDAY. AFTER THINKING ABOUT IT, HE CHANGES HIS MIND AND INSTEAD SUGGESTS GIVING HER:

a. A cake
b. Two cyanide tablets
c. A new pussy

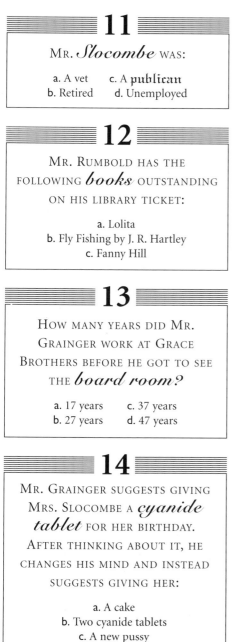

𝔭𝔲𝔟𝔩𝔦𝔠𝔞𝔫
proprietor of a pub

15

WHAT WAS MR. RUMBOLD'S FORMER *nickname* AND WHEN DID HE GET IT?

16

MRS. SLOCOMBE'S COUSIN RUNS A BREWERY IN IRELAND.

❑ *True* *False* ❑

17

IN AN EARLY EPISODE OF *GRACE AND FAVOUR*, MRS. SLOCOMBE CLAIMS SHE'S NEVER BEEN *in trouble* WITH THE LAW—IN ENGLAND, ANYWAY. HOW IS SHE PROVED WRONG A YEAR LATER?

18

IN WHICH *department* DID MR. RUMBOLD WORK PRIOR TO BECOMING MANAGER?

a. Hardware
b. Lingerie
c. Books

19

WHICH SPORT DOES *Captain Peacock* PLAY?

a. Cricket b. Darts
c. Skirt chasing d. Golf

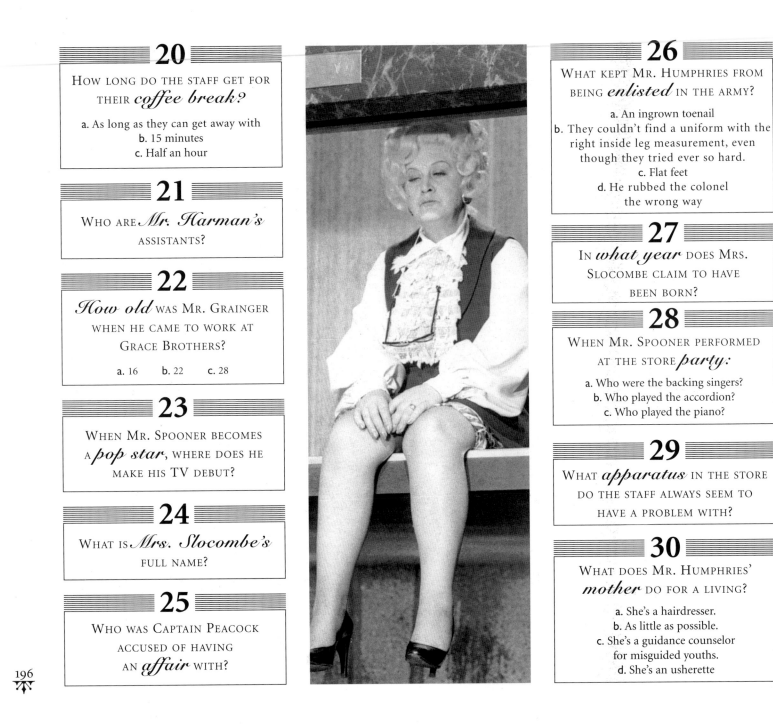

20
HOW LONG DO THE STAFF GET FOR THEIR *coffee break?*

a. As long as they can get away with
b. 15 minutes
c. Half an hour

21
WHO ARE *Mr. Harman's* ASSISTANTS?

22
How old WAS MR. GRAINGER WHEN HE CAME TO WORK AT GRACE BROTHERS?

a. 16   b. 22   c. 28

23
WHEN MR. SPOONER BECOMES A *pop star*, WHERE DOES HE MAKE HIS TV DEBUT?

24
WHAT IS *Mrs. Slocombe's* FULL NAME?

25
WHO WAS CAPTAIN PEACOCK ACCUSED OF HAVING AN *affair* WITH?

26
WHAT KEPT MR. HUMPHRIES FROM BEING *enlisted* IN THE ARMY?

a. An ingrown toenail
b. They couldn't find a uniform with the right inside leg measurement, even though they tried ever so hard.
c. Flat feet
d. He rubbed the colonel the wrong way

27
IN *what year* DOES MRS. SLOCOMBE CLAIM TO HAVE BEEN BORN?

28
WHEN MR. SPOONER PERFORMED AT THE STORE *party:*

a. Who were the backing singers?
b. Who played the accordion?
c. Who played the piano?

29
WHAT *apparatus* IN THE STORE DO THE STAFF ALWAYS SEEM TO HAVE A PROBLEM WITH?

30
WHAT DOES MR. HUMPHRIES' *mother* DO FOR A LIVING?

a. She's a hairdresser.
b. As little as possible.
c. She's a guidance counselor for misguided youths.
d. She's an usherette

31

ELSIE, DORIS, DAPHNE, EDITH, DEIRDRE, IVY, AND HILLARY ARE THE *names* OF:

a. Mrs. Slocombe's pussy's kittens
b. The cleaners at Grace Brothers
c. Aliases used by Mr. Humphries

32

WHAT ARE THE *hours* OF GRACE BROTHERS?

33

IN 1973, CAPTAIN PEACOCK HAS BEEN *married* FOR:

a. 14 years   b. 20 years   c. 24 years

34

VIA WHAT ROUTE THROUGH GRACE BROTHERS DID MR. GRAINGER ARRIVE IN *Men's Trousers?*

35

WHEN THE STAFF GO AWAY ON *holiday:*

a. Captain Peacock brings his wife.
   ❑ *True*   *False* ❑
b. Mr. Grainger brings his wife.
   ❑ *True*   *False* ❑
c. Mr. Humphries brings his wife.
   ❑ *True*   *False* ❑
d. Mr. Rumbold brings his wife.
   ❑ *True*   *False* ❑

36

WHICH *wives* LIVE AT MILLSTONE MANOR?

37

WHICH STAFF MEMBER WAS IN THE *Army Catering Corps?*

38

WHY DID MRS. SLOCOMBE SPEND SO MUCH OF THE WAR *on her back?*

39

WHICH FLOOR ARE THE GENTS' AND LADIES' *Ready-to-Wear* DEPARTMENTS ON?

a. First floor
b. Second floor
c. Third floor
d. Fourth floor

40

WHY DOESN'T MRS. SLOCOMBE NEED AN *alarm clock* TO GET UP IN THE MORNING?

41

HOW OLD WOULD MRS. SLOCOMBE'S PUSSY BE IN *animal years* WHEN THE STAFF MOVE TO MILLSTONE MANOR?

42

WHAT WAS *Mr. Grainger* GIVEN AT HIS RETIREMENT DINNER?

a. A gold watch
b. A combination shoe horn and back scratcher
c. A portrait of Young Mr. Grace

43

UNDER *what name* WAS MR. HUMPHRIES KNOWN DURING THE WAR?

a. Gladys Wanswright
b. Willy Buttable
c. Ben Dover

44

WHAT IS MRS. SLOCOMBE'S *earliest* MEMORY?

45

Mr. Rumbold WAS BORN IN 1934.

❏ *True*   *False* ❏

46

WHICH *movie* DOES MR. LUCAS TAKE MISS BRAHMS TO SEE?

a. Carnal Knowledge
b. Mary Poppins
c. The Unsatisfied Virgin

47

WHAT WAS THE *alternative?*

a. Bambi
b. The Sound of Music
c. Beneath the Valley of the Ultra Vixens

48

WHEN THE STAFF CELEBRATE MRS. SLOCOMBE'S *fiftieth birthday,* HOW OLD IS SHE REALLY?

49

WHICH *character* DOES MR. HUMPHRIES HAVE ON HIS WATCH?

a. Goofy
b. Pluto
c. Mickey Mouse

50

WHO ARE MR. LUCAS' *flatmates?*

51

DURING THE *war* MR. GRAINGER WAS IN ENSA. THIS WAS:

a. The entertainment corps
b. The catering corps
c. An acronym for Every Night Something Awful

52

HOW DID YOUNG MR. GRACE GET HIS *start?*

53

WHERE DOES MR. HUMPHRIES KEEP HIS *pajamas?*

a. Stuffed in his teddy bear
b. He doesn't own any.
c. In the fridge.

54

WHICH STAFF MEMBER IS REFERRED TO AS *"Jug Ears"?*

55

ACCORDING TO MRS. SLOCOMBE, WHAT ARE THE TWO TYPES OF *underwear?*

56

WHO USED TO WORK IN *Toys and Games* AND SOMETIMES PLAY WITH THE CHILDREN?

57

EARLY ON IN THE SERIES, MRS. SLOCOMBE IMPLIES HER HUSBAND *left her* RECENTLY. WHAT COMES OUT ABOUT HIS DEPARTURE IN *GRACE AND FAVOUR?*

58

WHO *runs off* WITH MR. RUMBOLD'S WIFE?

a. Mr. Patel of Accounts
b. Henry the Hairdresser
c. Mr. Prentice of Tools and Hardware
d. Mr. Walpole the Golf Pro

59

WHO *bites* CAPTAIN PEACOCK?

a. Miss Featherstone of Toiletries
b. Miss Aldenbrooke of Accounts
c. Miss Robinson of Jewelry
d. Mr. Chamberlain of China and Glass

60

WHERE DOES *Mr. Lucas* KEEP HIS PAJAMAS?

61

WHAT DOES MISS BRAHMS TAKE
TO *bed* WITH HER?

62

AFTER MRS. SLOCOMBE IS GIVEN
EARLY RETIREMENT AND BEFORE
SHE IS REINSTATED, SHE *returns*
TO GRACE BROTHERS AS A:

a. Floor cleaner
b. Waitress
c. Window cleaner

63

MR. HUMPHRIES' MOTHER GETS
ABOUT IN A *motorbike*
AND SIDECAR.

❏ *True*   *False* ❏

64

WHAT IS *next door* TO
GRACE BROTHERS?

a. Wimpy Burgers
b. Marks and Spencers
c. The Oklahoma Pancake House
d. Beppo's

65

DOES MISS BRAHMS EVER *kiss*
MR. HUMPHRIES IN *ARE YOU
BEING SERVED?*

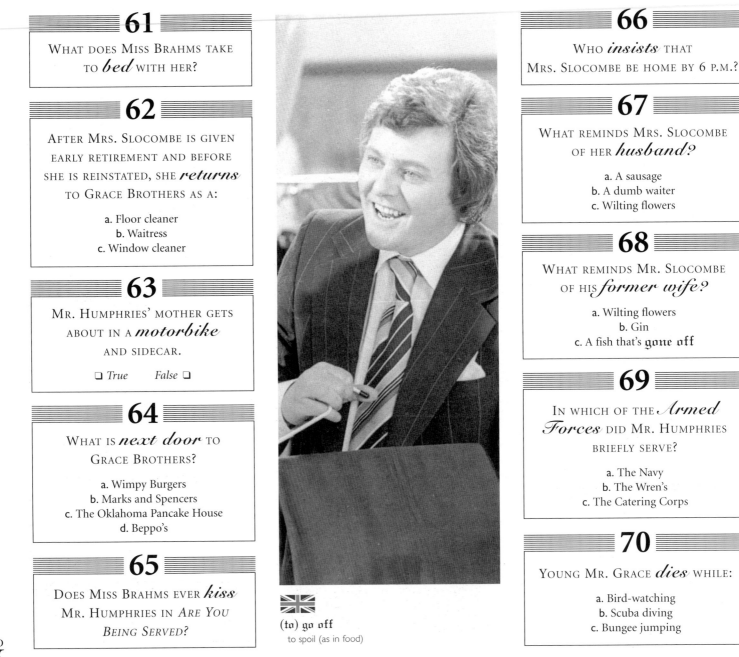

🇬🇧
(to) go off
to spoil (as in food)

66

WHO *insists* THAT
MRS. SLOCOMBE BE HOME BY 6 P.M.?

67

WHAT REMINDS MRS. SLOCOMBE
OF HER *husband?*

a. A sausage
b. A dumb waiter
c. Wilting flowers

68

WHAT REMINDS MR. SLOCOMBE
OF HIS *former wife?*

a. Wilting flowers
b. Gin
c. A fish that's **gone off**

69

IN WHICH OF THE *Armed
Forces* DID MR. HUMPHRIES
BRIEFLY SERVE?

a. The Navy
b. The Wren's
c. The Catering Corps

70

YOUNG MR. GRACE *dies* WHILE:

a. Bird-watching
b. Scuba diving
c. Bungee jumping

71

THE FOLLOWING *items* OF CLOTHING MUST BE WORN BY GRACE BROTHERS' FEMALE EMPLOYEES:

a. Grace Brothers' blouses
❏ *True*   *False* ❏

b. Stockings and tights
❏ *True*   *False* ❏

c. Grace Brothers' name tags
❏ *True*   *False* ❏

72

WHAT CAN *senior staff* AT GRACE BROTHERS DO THAT JUNIOR STAFF CANNOT?

73

WHICH STAFF MEMBER'S IDEAL HOLIDAY SPOT IS A *nudist colony* ON LEVANT?

a. Mr. Humphries
b. Mr. Lucas
c. Captain Peacock

74

ONE OF MR. RUMBOLD'S SECRETARIES HAD A NAME THAT RHYMED WITH A FAMOUS LONDON *department store.*

HER NAME WAS:

a. Miss Belfridge
b. Miss Barrods
c. Miss Bimpsons

75

WHO DIDN'T ATTEND THE READING OF YOUNG MR. GRACE'S *will?*

76

MISS BRAHMS' FIRST NAME IS *Joanne.*

❏ *True*   *False* ❏

77

WHOSE *catchphrase* IS "YOU'VE ALL DONE VERY WELL"?

78

Mr. Grainger's
FIRST NAME IS:

a. Winston
b. Ernest
c. Herman

79

Captain Peacock's
FIRST NAME IS:

a. Stephen
b. Jeremy
c. Horace

80

Who IS ALWAYS "UNANIMOUS"?

81

IN THE *advert* FOR GRACE BROTHERS' CLUB RENDEZ-VOUS:

a. Who is Pierre the Chef?
b. Who wears a top hat and tails?
c. Who dresses as a maid?
d. Who wears a bunny outfit?
e. Who is a doorman without a door?

82

WHO IS MRS. SLOCOMBE'S *neighbor?*

83

WHO IS *Assistant 134?*

84

WHERE DID MR. SLOCOMBE GO *every morning* AT 9:30?

a. To work
b. To feed the ducks
c. To bet on the horses

85

AT THE MALE AND FEMALE MODES ON THE *Move* FASHION SHOW:

a. Who wears an outfit inspired by James Bond in *You Only Live Twice?*
b. Who are ready to jump into bed together?
c. Who takes her inspiration from The Pallisers?
d. Who plays Rodney, the city tycoon?

86

WHY DOES MR. GRAINGER'S DOCTOR ADVISE HIM TO *give up* HIS FAVORITE SPORT?

87

WHO WROTE THE *theme music* FOR *ARE YOU BEING SERVED?*

88

WHAT SIZE *collar* DOES CAPTAIN PEACOCK WEAR?

89

WHY IS *August 3,* 1953, SO SIGNIFICANT FOR MR. GRAINGER?

90

HOW WAS CAPTAIN PEACOCK *injured* DURING THE SUEZ CAMPAIGN?

a. A grenade exploded near him.
b. He fell out of his bed while having a nightmare.
c. He cut himself while shaving.

91

WHAT DOES MR. RUMBOLD *cuddle* WITH IN BED?

a. A red koala bear
b. His pillow
c. His wife

92

GRACE BROTHERS STAFF MAY NOT USE THE *public toilets.*

❑ True   False ❑

93

GRACE BROTHERS *owns:*

a. The His and Hers Perfume Company
b. The Wharfside Coke Company
c. The Whirlybird Travel Agency

94

WHEN IS THE ONLY TIME MR. HARMAN REMEMBERS HE IS *not allowed* ON THE FLOOR DURING WORKING HOURS?

95

MR. HUMPHRIES' MOTHER MOVED IN WITH HIM IN 1976, THE EXCUSE BEING THAT SHE HAD ꞃoweꝺ WITH HIS FATHER. WHAT IN LATER EPISODES MAKES THIS EXCUSE *questionable?*

🇬🇧
(tʊ) rʊw
to argue

96

WHEN BURGLARS *attack* GRACE BROTHERS:

a. Who pretend to be policemen?
b. Who wears a zoot suit and pretends to be Pa Gumby?
c. Who poses as mad Ma Gumby?
d. Who plays the infamous womanizer Italian Tony?

97

DURING MR. HUMPHRIES' BRIEF STINT IN THE NAVY, HE ONCE WENT ASHORE WEARING THE *Captain's cap* AND HIS TROUSERS.

❑ True   False ❑

98

How many SALES DID MR. LUCAS MAKE IN THE MONTH BEFORE "OUR FIGURES ARE SLIPPING"?

a. 3   b. 13   c. 30

99

WHAT IS THE *first thing* MR. LUCAS IS TAUGHT BY CAPTAIN PEACOCK?

100

WHICH STAFF MEMBER DOES NOT WEAR A *vest?*

203

Answers

TO THE
TRIVIA QUESTIONS

What Your Score Suggests

100 CORRECT ANSWERS:
You must be one of the writers of *Are You Being Served?* Or you've cheated.

90 TO 99 CORRECT ANSWERS:
You've watched each episode every time it has been aired and think about little else.

80 TO 89 CORRECT ANSWERS:
You have a very good memory. Or you guess well on tests.

70 TO 79 CORRECT ANSWERS:
You've missed a number of episodes. Or you're missing a number of memory cells. Or both.

60 TO 69 CORRECT ANSWERS:
You've watched the show for the wrong reasons.

FEWER THAN 60 CORRECT ANSWERS:
You call yourself a fan?

1. b.

2. Mr. Grainger joined Grace Brothers' staff.

3. b.

4. That's when his mother locks the doors.

5. c.

6. They're both false—it's the other way around.

7. 1567.

8. c) She uses her many charms on him.

9. Tiddles.

10. His mother put him out by mistake instead of the cat.

11. d.

12. All of them.

13. c.

14. b.

15. Knuckles. He was once in a roller-skating gang accused of stealing two grapefruits and a cox's orange pippin (an apple) from a Romford shop in 1946.

16. False; she runs a farm in Scotland.

17. Her police record shows she has a long history of clashes with policemen, including the time a policeman immobilized her in Blackpool, and another time when she knocked the helmet off a policeman in Soho.

18. a.

19. d.

20. b.

21. Henry and Seymour.

22. c.

23. On *Around London*, a (fictitious) local TV news program.

24. Mrs. Mary Elizabeth (Betty) Jennifer Rachel Yiddell Abergavenny Slocombe.

25. Miss Hazelwood, Mr. Rumbold's secretary.

26. a.

27. 1930.

28. a) Miss Brahms and Mrs. Slocombe; b) Mr. Rumbold; c) Captain Peacock.

29. The lift.

30. d.

31. b.

32. 9 a.m. until 5:30 p.m.

33. a.

34. Haberdashery to Stationery to Bathroom Furnishings to Gentlemen's Shoes to Gentlemen's Trousers.

35. They're all false; not one brought his wife—especially Mr. Humphries, who doesn't have one.

36. None.

37. Mr. Rumbold.

38. She was pinned down by air raids—or so she says.

39. a (in early episodes of the series); b (in the film); c (in the Australian version); d (in later episodes).

40. Her pussy drops its clockwork mouse on her pillow every morning at 6:15 a.m.

41. More than 150 years old.

42. b.

43. a.

44. Of an uncle sticking his red face into her cot.

45. False; he was born in 1924.

46. c.

47. a.

48. 46.

49. c.

50. His crippled mother, who used to work in a skating rink, an asthmatic cat, and an Asian lodger—or so he tells Mr. Rumbold when he's in trouble.

51. a, c.

52. Running a fish stall.

53. a.

54. Mr. Rumbold.

55. Cold and Interesting; Warm and Safe.

56. Captain Peacock.

57. That he's been gone for 40 years.

58. c.

59. b.

60. In Basil Brush, a glove-puppet fox with buck teeth (Basil brush was also a TV show popular with children).

61. A Donald Duck hot water bottle.

62. a, b, c.

63. True.

64. c, d.

65. Yes, in "The Hold-Up," to persuade the burglars that Mr. Humphries is really Italian Tony, the infamous womanizer.

66. Her pussy.

67. c.

68. b.

69. a.

70. b.

71. a) false; b) true; c) false.

72. Smoke cigars.

73. c.

74. a.

75. Mr. Rumbold, because he's managing Millstone Manor.

76. False; her name is Shirley.

77. Young Mr. Grace.

78. b.

79. a

80. Mrs. Slocombe.

81. a) Mr. Humphries; b) Mr. Harman and Mr. Rumbold; c) Miss Brahms; d) the canteen manageress; e) Mr. Spooner.

82. Mr. Akbar.

83. Miss Brahms.

84. b.

85. a) Mr. Humphries; b) Miss Brahms and Mr. Grainger, alias Tania and Tony; c) Mrs. Slocombe as Naomi; d) Captain Peacock.

86. Because of his back.

87. Ronnie Hazlehurst, a prominent composer for British sitcoms, though he was never credited on any episode.

88. 15 1/2.

89. He and his wife had sex that day.

90. c.

91. a.

92. True.

93. a, b.

94. When Captain Peacock asks him to contribute to the collection for Mrs. Slocombe's birthday present.

95. Doubts about her son's parentage.

96. a) Captain Peacock and Mr. Spooner; b) Mr. Harman; c) Mrs. Slocombe; d) Mr. Humphries.

97. He was wearing the cap—but not the trousers.

98. a.

99. The proper way to fold his handkerchief.

100. Mr. Lucas.

British Terms

advert
advertisement

backing singers
back-up singers

bee's knees
the hottest thing going, as in "in his time he was the bee's knees"

bird
a woman

biscuits
cookies, when referred to as "sweet biscuits" or "tea biscuits"; plain biscuit (used, for example, to serve with cheese) often refers to crackers

bloomer
embarrassing mistake

a blow
a try, as in "to give someone a blow at something"

a blow at the organ
a pump of the organ's bellows

bouncer
in the sport of cricket, a short-pitched ball delivery that goes about head high to the batsman; also, in popular slang, a woman's breasts

(to) bowl
in the sport of cricket, to throw the ball to a batsman, the equivalent of baseball's pitching

(to) call forward
to call over

(to) call round
to pay a visit, drop over

cart
garbage truck

chat shows
talk shows

(to) chat up
to sweet-talk or try to convince someone (usually a member of the opposite sex) of something; to come on to

chemist
pharmacy (also a pharmacist)

Christmas crackers
novelty items sold during the holiday season; fancily wrapped cardboard cylinders that are pulled from both ends, making a snapping or "cracking" sound when the wrapping tears off and revealing toys, candy, or other small trinkets inside; also, rhyming slang for knackers, or testicles

concert party
a group of traveling soldiers—usually actors before conscription—who put on musical and comedy performances for troops at various military installations during wartime; also applies to such groups that perform seasonally, moving from place to place

corpsing
committing any of a number of stage gaffes, including breaking into laughter, making a mistake in one's lines, spoiling a scene, or forgetting one's lines

cot
baby's crib

207

council
> local authorities who organize services—such as garbage collection—employing staff to do so; specifically borough council, county council, parish council; in 1970s sitcoms council workers were often portrayed as lazy

daft
> flighty or silly

diarist
> columnist

dicky
> shirt collar

dodgy
> tricky, risky

dogsbody (or dog's body)
> gofer, low person in company hierarchy

double act
> a performance by two people, à la Burns & Allen

down at heel
> down and out

dressing down
> a reprimand

(to) drop oneself in it
> to get oneself into trouble

drying
> completely forgetting one's lines

duff
> substandard, inferior

dustbinman
> garbage collector, also dustman

duty office
> audience services office

electric fire
> an electric heater

end-of-the-pier
> off-color or risqué, as in "end-of-the-pier humor"

(to) engage someone
> to hire someone, as in "he engaged a private secretary"

(to) fancy
> to like, desire, as in "he fancies that woman in the corner" or "I fancy tea and biscuits just now"; to fancy oneself is to have a large ego

a few buttons short of a waistcoat
> dull, unintelligent; same as American expression "a few cards short of a full deck"

fruit machine
> slot machine, gambling machine, one-armed bandit

(to) get into bed with
> to join up with, become partners with

(to) get struck off
> to have one's license removed, especially with regard to a physician whose name has been taken off the medical registry

(to) give the boot
> to fire from a job

(to) go off
> to spoil (as in food)

gob-smacked
> shocked or angered into speechlessness

grace and favour
> an expression used in connection with a piece of property (such as an apartment or small cottage) and referring to rent-free occupancy awarded to a retired loyal retainer, royal or otherwise

(to) holiday
> to go on vacation

a Jack-the-lad
> one who is the most conspicuous in a group, usually a charming troublemaker

(to) kip
> to (go to) sleep

(to) knee (a men's jacket)
> a fitting technique whereby a tight garment is made roomier by breaking some stitches by stretching it across a knee

knickers
ladies' underpants

launderette
laundromat

a leg up
a boost, a means of assistance

lift
elevator

(to) lift
to steal

lorry
truck

mackintosh or mac
raincoat

main chance
a big break

mate
an assistant or apprentice; also, a good friend

maths
mathematics, as in "he nearly flunked his maths"

McGill postcards
stylized seaside postcards by an artist named McGill featuring illustrations of large-breasted women, skinny men, and captions rife with double entendres

mincing
dainty, only affectedly so

motoring
driving

Mr. Kipling
one of Britain's leading manufacturers of dessert cakes and biscuits, a (nonexistent) character brought to life in advertisements

(to) muck in
to help out or pitch in

(to) muck up
to make a mess of things

Naafi
an Armed Forces canteen, acronym of Navy, Army, and Air Force Institutes; the enterprise (like the American PX) that maintains canteens and service centers for British Armed Forces personnel

National Service
military service

not up to scratch
unacceptable

OBE
Order of the British Empire; one of the honorary titles given to a British subject and awarded on the monarch's birthday, on New Year's Day, or at the time of a prime minister's resignation

(to call or have) on the carpet
to receive a reprimand

one-off
done or performed only once, as in a "one-off play"; also, referring to something manufactured, a one-of-a-kind item

Page Three Girl
a model who has appeared in topless pin-ups on page three of Britain's tabloid newspapers

pantomime
a show produced during the Christmas season, usually based on fairy tales or ancient legends, which incorporates singing, dancing, and, most notably, very broad humor

pay rise
pay raise

(to) pinch
to steal

posh
elegant, first-class, often pretentiously so

potato crisps (or crisps)
potato chips

publican
proprietor of a pub

pudding
dessert, as in "What kind of pudding do you want after dinner?"

(to) queue up
to stand in line (to wait for something)

racing saloon cars
sports cars of some 30 to 40 years ago when sports cars were souped up saloon (or sedan) cars and little different from racing cars

redundancies, to make redundant
layoffs, to lay off

rota
people acting in turn, one after another

round the twist
(also round the bend) crazy, as in "to drive someone round the twist"

(to) row
to argue

royal walkabout
a public stroll taken by the monarch or other member of the Royal Family

(to) sack
to fire (as from a job)

sarky
sarcastic

(to) send up
to make fun of or do a humorous "takeoff" on someone or something

skip
large trash container

sporran
in traditional Scottish dress, a small pouch or purse that is hung from the front of one's belt

squatter
one who inhabits an apartment, building, or land (which is often public or otherwise unclaimed) without official title or lease

starter
appetizer before main course of meal

steel sink
servant's sink, kitchen sink, as distinguished from a porcelain sink, which would be found in the upstairs master's quarters

(to) stock-take
to take inventory of merchandise

straight away
immediately, instantly

(to) take the mickey out of
to make fun of

(to) tear him off a strip
to criticize, probably derived from the military, referring to demotion (removing an officer's stripes)

think tank
a gathering of (supposedly) intelligent people who compare ideas on a topic and then come up with a plan on how to proceed; as in "they hold a think tank"

3d
threepence (pronounced "thruppence"), referring to a pre-decimal coin or monetary unit—240 of them in a pound—where pence (or penny) was abbreviated as d; comes from *denarius* (a Roman coin having the lowest monetary value)

throw up
give up, quit, as in "he threw up his day job"

till
cash register

twit
a jerk

up to scratch
acceptable

voice-off
voiceover

want to know
have a use or need for, as in "they didn't want to know me"

washing powder
laundry detergent

washing-up
dishwashing

wide boy
one who lives by his wits; a questionable or shady character

ADRIAN RIGELSFORD, A WRITER AND ACTOR, lives in Cambridgeshire, England. His books include: *The Doctors-30 Years of Time Travel, Doctor Who-Monsters, The Turquoise Mountain, The Dynamite Kid* (these two written with Brian Blessed), *Doctor Who-Cybermen, The Blake Chronicles,* and *The Film Review Year Book.* His film and television credits include: *Galahad of Everest, The Abominable Snowmen, Sons of the Desert, Frankenstein, Cabby,* and many other productions.

ANTHONY BROWN IS A LONG-STANDING TELLY addict who turned to writing after studying engineering and mathematics at London's Imperial College and the University of East Anglia, where he worked at the campus TV station. A science fiction fan, he edited the telefantasy magazine *DWB* from 1993 to 1994, but has become more interested in television in general in recent years. He has helped out on books covering a number of TV series, but *Are You Being Served?—The Inside Story* is the first book on which he has formally collaborated. He lives in Essex, England.

GEOFF TIBBALLS BECAME A FULL-TIME AUTHOR in 1989 after working in television for 15 years. He has since published more than 20 books, including *The Encyclopedia of TV Detectives,* the widely acclaimed history of television *Box of Delights,* and a number of other TV-related books, among them best-selling tie-ins to *London's Burning, Soldier Soldier, Brookside, The Big Breakfast,* and *Taggart.* He lives in Nottingham with his wife, two daughters, and an ageing cat.

EVERY COMMUNITY ACROSS AMERICA IS REACHED by one of the 346 member stations of the Public Broadcasting Service. These stations provide information, entertainment, and insight for the whole family.

Think about the programs you enjoy and remember most:

*Mystery…Masterpiece Theatre…Nova…Nature…Sesame Street…Ghostwriter …Reading Rainbow…Baseball…The Civil War…MacNeil/Lehrer News Hour… Great Performances…Washington Week in Review…*and so many more.

On your local PBS station, you'll also find fascinating adult education courses, provocative documentaries, great cooking and do-it-yourself programs, and thoughtful local analysis.

Despite the generous underwriting contributions of foundations and corporations, more than half of all public televsion budgets comes from individual member support.

For less than the cost of a night at the movies, less than a couple of months of a daily paper, less than a month of your cable TV bill, you can help make possible all the quality programming you enjoy.

Become a member of your public broadcasting station and do your part.

Public Television. You make it happen!